MUCH IS REQUIRED

by

Grant Sweeney

Grosvenor House
Publishing Limited

This book is published by
Grosvenor House Publishing Ltd
Link House
140 The Broadway, Tolworth, Surrey, KT6 7HT.
www.grosvenorhousepublishing.co.uk

This book is a work of fiction. Any resemblance to
people or events, past or present, is purely coincidental.

A CIP record for this book
is available from the British Library

ISBN 978-1-80381-948-8

For Gary & Dawn
My perfect parents

Contents

1

The austere darkness and heavy silence surrounding The Puppet Master Hotel were broken only by the approach of a lone car's headlights reflecting off the pavement. The worn 2014 Volvo V40 glided into the nearly vacant parking area, claiming a spot beside a humble Ford Fiesta, roughly twenty yards from the looming hotel entrance.

Within the cosy warmth of the idling car, Shell Kingham surveyed the shadowy facade before her with bloodshot eyes that betrayed many sleepless nights. Her long raven hair lifted up by a loose bobble, contrasting the thick layers she wore for protection against the autumn chill.

Traces of yesterday's makeup still clung to her weary face, hinting she rarely had time for such trivial routines. Though small in stature, everything about her posture and expression suggested she could erupt with aggressive energy if provoked.

Rummaging through the clutter of her passenger seat, Shell retrieved a weathered journal from her handbag with an ink pen dangling from its binding. She jotted a new entry about halfway through the volume, the pages dense with cramped handwriting.

"Just arrived at The Puppet Master Hotel in Aston by Sutton. It's now Friday 10th October at roughly 7:30pm. I don't know how this is gonna go, but I know this is the closest I've ever been to discovering the truth. I fear this might be my final entry but I've left everything I know in here for you to investigate, so please - if anything happens to me tonight, do something with this journal, I beg of you ... But just to be on the safe side, my full name is Michelle Kingham. I live with my dad, Michael, in Lime Grove in Liverpool, I'm 33 ... and I'm Mark Kingham's sister. – Luke 12:48."

Shell returned the weathered journal to her handbag and flipped off the glaring dome light, embracing the solitude as she stepped out into the biting wind, taking the handbag with her. She clicked her car locked and marched with purpose toward the doors.

Muffled voices echoed from the hotel's entrance, barely audible over the whispering wind. Shell cinched her handbag tighter as she draped the strap over her right shoulder and strode toward the doors, the tapping of her boots punctuating the stillness.

Warm air washed over her as she stepped inside. Rounding the corner, she spotted the front desk and ambled over, pausing as a heated exchange grabbed her attention.

The female receptionist sat rigid, tight lipped as two men loomed over her at her desk, alcohol heavy on their breath. Shell assessed them quickly - disheveled clothes, unkempt hair, swaying slightly on their feet. Trouble.

"Yes, I know, sir, but—" the receptionist attempted, her eyes flitting to Shell, desperation in her gaze. "If your friend can't pay for the two nights he's already stayed here, I'll have to call security!"

"I mean, he's not done anything wrong though, he's skint," the taller man slurred. "Come on, it's freezing out there. Are you really gonna kick someone out who's homeless?"

Shell hovered nearby, senses heightened. Her hand drifted casually to her handbag.

As the tirade between the receptionist and the tall man ensued, the stockier man noticed Shell's approach, an ugly leer twisting his lips.

"Hey, don't I know you?" His glance raked down her body. Shell didn't respond. "I bet you're a right filthy slag, aren't you? Fancy a fuck?"

Shell tensed, bile rising in her throat. Her fist closed around the zipper on her handbag. "If you don't get out of my face in the next three seconds, I'm pepper spraying you both!"

The receptionist hurried over in solidarity, having stopped explaining to the taller man why he and his friend were no longer welcomed guests of the hotel. "Right, that's it! Get the fuck out!" the woman yelled, jabbing a finger toward the exit. "Security are on their way!"

The taller man grabbed his crass friend's arm, muttering apologies as he yanked him away. Their protests faded as they exited the building.

Shell loosened her white-knuckled grip on her bag, pulse still hammering. "Are you alright?"

The receptionist sighed, weariness etched on her face. "Yeah. I'm sorry about that. I can't stand this job sometimes." She moved unsteadily back to her station.

Composing herself, Shell stepped up to the desk. "It's fine, they're gone now."

"Yeah, thank you. How can I help?"

"I have a reservation under Michelle Kingham for Room 48."

Having regained her professional attitude, the receptionist tapped at her keyboard. "Ah yes. Single room, one night?". Shell nodded.

The receptionist grabbed a keycard from the shelf beneath the desk and passed it over to Shell. "Top floor, end of the hall on your left. The Wi-Fi password is on the card. Let me know if you need anything else."

Shell thanked her and turned toward the nearby stairwell doors, keycard in hand.

"Michelle?"

Shell glanced over her shoulder. "Yeah?"

"Thank you for helping me out with those guys," sincerity shone in her eyes. "I don't know what would've happened if you hadn't turned up when you did."

The corner of Shell's mouth quirked. "Don't worry about it. Have a good night."

Pushing through the heavy doors, Shell climbed upwards on the hardened stairs, accompanied by her echoing footsteps. She reached the top floor and walked briskly along the hallway. The floral-patterned carpet muffled each step she took.

As Shell neared the peeling door of Room 41, it suddenly swung open, its shrieking hinges would have startled a ghost in a haunted castle.

Shell jumped back as a young man in his early twenties hurried from the room, nearly colliding with her.

"Oh God, I'm so sorry!" the young man exclaimed, throwing out a hand to steady himself against the wall.

Shell pressed a palm to her thudding heart, sucking in a sharp breath, composing herself. Adrenaline still coursed through her veins as she met the young man's concerned gaze. "It's okay." she assured him.

The young man ran an agitated hand through his mussed brown hair. "Are you alright?" he asked anxiously. "I didn't see you there. I'm running late and wasn't expecting anyone outside my door. I'm really sorry!"

"Just bad timing," Shell said. She offered him a timid smile, hoping to set him at ease. "I'm fine, don't worry. Go on."

"Okay, again—I'm really sorry." The young man backed away awkwardly, then turned and headed for the stairs, moving briskly but taking care not to appear as if he were fleeing the scene.

Shell watched the young man descend out of sight before gathering herself and continuing down the hallway.

As she neared Room 48, she couldn't resist glancing over her shoulder at Room 47 directly across from her.

A strange sense of foreboding trickled down her spine. Shaking it off, she unlocked the door and entered her temporary sanctuary.

The furnishings of Shell's room were plain and worn, the floral bedspread faded with age. She perched tentatively on the edge of the bed, gripping her handbag.

After a moment, Shell reached inside and retrieved an old Nokia phone. Rising abruptly, she shoved the phone into her pocket. Next she pulled out a ring box and flipped it open with trembling fingers. Nestled inside was a gold ring engraved with the words "*United Kingham*."

Tears blurred Shell's vision as she reverently lifted the ring from its satin bed. Clutching it tightly to her pounding heart, she blinked back the moisture in her eyes.

Slipping the empty box into her bag, Shell strode to the door with a new purpose.

Exiting the room, she gazed down while pulling the door shut with a definitive click. Taking a steadying breath, Shell focused on the door of Room 47. She stood mere inches away, working up her nerve.

Finally, she raised a fist and rapped firmly on the scarred wood. Faint sounds of movement whispered from within.

Shell knocked again, more insistently this time. "Lee?" she called, her voice echoing slightly in the empty hall. "Lee Barker?"

A faint scuffling sound came from behind the door, as if someone pressed themselves against the wood. When a timid voice spoke up, the noise stopped.

"Yeah?" The man's voice was muffled by the barrier between them.

"My name is Shell. We've never met before, but...can I come in, please?" Shell's words tumbled out in a rush. "We need to talk."

A brief silence. "What about?" His tone held a note of suspicion.

Shell wet her lips, grasping for the right words. "A lot of things. Please? Open the door."

More silence. Shell shifted from foot to foot, nerves making her chest tight.

Finally, the man responded. "I'm sorry, but I'm not opening the door," his voice hardened. "Go away."

Jaw tightening, Shell opened her palm, gazing down at the engraved gold ring resting there. Crouching, she slid the ring under the gap beneath the door. As she rose, a shocked gasp came from within, followed by the soft scooping of the ring off the floor.

"Shell?" Disbelief coloured the man's voice. "You're Shell Kingham?"

"Yeah."

The door swung inward.

At last. Shell found herself face-to-face with 37 year old Lee Barker.

Lee looked disheveled, his skin sagging as if he had once carried a substantial amount of weight he had since lost. His light-coloured, shabby clothes accompanied a cheap watch attached to his left wrist, and his feet were clad only in black socks. What little hair he had left clung to his scalp in wispy patches. Lee clutched the gold ring in his right hand, holding it up by his chest.

"Where did you get this?" His eyes were narrowed with suspicion.

"You know where." Shell said simply.

Lee's gaze darted down the hall, movements jittery. "No. No, he can't be here. He's come for me, hasn't he?" His breathing quickened. "I knew it, I knew it—"

"I came alone," Shell interjected firmly. "No one's with me, calm down."

Lee briefly examined her stern facial expression. "Prove it."

Shell frowned. "What?"

"You heard."

"How?"

Lee considered this momentarily. "How did you get here?"

"I drove."

"You've parked outside?"

"Yes."

Lee nodded sharply. "Okay. Go back to your car. Make it look like you're leaving...I'll watch from my window. If I see Mark or anyone else with you, don't bother coming back up."

Frustration mounting, Shell bit back a sharp retort. "Lee, I don't have time for this."

He met her gaze challengingly. With a huff, Shell threw up her hands. "You want me to just go and sit in my car?"

"Yes, only for a few seconds."

Shell rolled her eyes. "Fine."

Lee's shoulders relaxed marginally. "Just so I can be sure."

"Alright," Shell bit out. She turned on her heels then strode purposefully along the hallway, hearing Lee's door slamming shut before she reached the stairs.

The receptionist sat at the large wooden desk in the hotel lobby, gazing absentmindedly at her computer screen. Her reverie was interrupted as the heavy double doors suddenly swung open and Shell came bursting through.

Shell's eyes were wild, her chest heaving from exertion. Wisps of her hair had escaped from her loose bobble and clung to the sweat on her forehead. In her haste, she nearly knocked over a decorative table in the lobby. The young receptionist straightened up in surprise.

"Is everything okay?" she asked hesitantly.

Shell called over her shoulder, already halfway across the lobby, "Yeah, yeah - just left something in the car, won't be a sec." She breezed through the main doors back out into the night.

A blast of cold air hit Shell's flushed cheeks as she hurried across the car park. The tarmac glistened due to a shroud of light rain, which reflected the harsh yellow lights from the lampposts. Her breath came out in frosty puffs. With trembling hands she dug through her bag for her keys, finally retrieving them and hitting the unlock button.

Shell opened the car door and slid into the driver's seat. Her heart pounded. Her throat felt dry and tight.

Bathed in the dim glow of the interior light, Shell slowly raised her eyes. From this vantage point, she had a clear view of the upper floor of the hotel. Most of the rooms were dark at this hour, but she could see a shadowy figure standing in one window, staring down at her intently. Lee was clearly keeping a close eye on Shell's surroundings.

A feeling of unease twisted her gut. She forced herself to take a deep breath before turning away and rifling through the contents of the glove box opposite the passenger seat.

Shell grabbed a small leather-bound book and quickly switched off the interior light. Clutching the book in one hand, she stepped out and locked the car door before hurrying back toward the hotel.

Shell kept her eyes trained upward. Lee's dark figure still stood sentinel in the window, features obscured by the glass and distance. She felt the weight of his gaze following her as she stepped back into the warmth of the lobby.

"All sorted now," she said to the receptionist, forcing a smile to cover her nerves. Shell slipped the book into her bag - a bible, if anyone bothered to look closely - before making her way to the lifts.

The receptionist appeared slightly reassured, but Shell would not blame her if she was still reeling from her earlier encounter with the two drunken louts.

Stepping out of the barely functioning lift onto the quiet top floor hallway, Shell steeled herself as she walked towards Lee's room.

Time to get some answers.

Shell raised her fist and knocked sharply on the door of Room 47.

2

Shell stood outside Lee's door, shoulders stiff with tension, and rapped her knuckles against the wood once more.

A few seconds passed before the door swung open. Lee looked at her expectantly.

"Satisfied?" Shell asked, tone clipped.

Lee stepped back wordlessly. Shell strode into the room, scanning her surroundings as Lee eased the door closed behind them.

The space was small and cramped, with peeling paint and threadbare carpet that had seen better days. A single bed took up most of the room, two large gym bags placed atop the rumpled sheets. The rest of the furnishings were similarly sparse - just a rickety chair tucked into one corner, a tiny bathroom alcove, and a small waste bin by the bathroom door.

Shell shuffled further inside, movements cautious, as if entering unfamiliar territory - which, in a way, she was.

"Do you wanna sit down?" Lee gestured limply to the chair, the gold ring still firmly grasped in his right hand.

"Not just yet, thanks."

Lee lowered himself to perch stiffly on the edge of the bed. His fingers worried at a loose bit of skin around his thumb as he watched Shell pace the length of the room. She paused by the window, scanning the car park below.

"Where are you parked?" she asked.

"It's the Ford Fiesta on the far right. Next to your car."

"It's actually my dad's," she murmured. "You're renting that Fiesta, yeah?"

"Yeah. For the week." Lee said, matter of factly.

Shell turned from the window and faced him fully. Lee shifted under the intensity of her stare.

"Okay, Lee," Her voice was steady despite the apprehension in her eyes. "How many nights have you stayed here so far?"

"Here, as in…"

"Aston, and this hotel."

Lee wet his lips. His leg jiggled restlessly. "Well, I stayed in a B&B down the road the first night. Been at The Puppet Master for two nights now. I'm here until Sunday."

Shell nodded, slow and deliberate. "That checks out. Thank you for being honest with me."

Lee huffed softly. "Oh. You already knew."

"Yeah," A humourless smile tugged at Shell's mouth. "I need to trust you, otherwise there's no point in me being here, is there?"

"Fair enough."

Shell resumed her pacing, shoes scuffing against the thin carpet. "I've done my research, Lee. You, of all people, should understand that."

Lee's expression was unreadable. "I do. I understand."

"Good," Shell stilled, facing him with fists planted on her hips. "Now I'll sit."

She retrieved the chair from the corner and set it directly across from Lee. Shell wasn't sure about the sturdiness of the chair. It definitely belonged in the bottom of a skip somewhere. How it ended up in a hotel, she'll never know. Nevertheless, as she sat down, settling her handbag on her lap, Lee spoke up.

"Before you ask anything else...could you tell me how you found me?" He gave a weak, conciliatory smile. "If that's alright?"

Shell returned his gaze evenly. "Sure. I suppose that's fair." She leaned back slightly in her seat, crossing one leg over the other.

"You were really clever those first eighteen months or so - I'll give you that - but you've been really sloppy lately. You used to switch up hotels and fake names constantly. But the past few months?" Shell made a scornful noise in the back of her throat. "Top floor, corner room, every single time. Plus, all your aliases had the initials M.K. Did you think me and my dad wouldn't notice?"

Lee stared down at the gold ring in his hand, saying nothing.

"I took a chance showing up in Sunderland two weeks ago, but there you were. Didn't take much to trail you after that. I carried on writing down how many nights you'd stay in one place before moving onto the next," Shell gave a careless shrug. "Wasn't difficult, really."

Silence reigned. Lee continued studying the ring, brow furrowed. After a long moment he spoke, voice hushed.

"So...when did Mark give you this?"

Shell's gaze was fixed to Lee's hand, more specifically to the gold ring. "Last time I saw him."

"Was he angry?"

The question seemed to startle Shell. She recoiled slightly. "No. He always said that you had nothing to do with it."

At that, Lee straightened. Something like pride flickered across his face.

"He said that?"

"Yeah."

Lee exhaled in a rush. "He's right though. I had nothing to do with what happened."

Shell's expression shuttered. "So I've heard."

The barest hint of a smile teased Lee's mouth. He reached down and carefully tucked the gold ring into his unzipped trouser pocket, movements reverent.

After he closed the zip on the pocket, Lee raised his eyes to Shell's. There was something urgent in them she hadn't noticed until then. Something vulnerable.

"He talked about you all the time, you know. Never showed me any pictures, but the way he spoke..." Lee trailed off, shaking his head. "Well. I could picture exactly how you looked."

The silence swelled between them once more. Shell shifted in her seat.

"Mark is my best friend, always has been. He's like the brother I never had."

"He's *my* brother, Lee."

"Right. Of course," Lee rubbed the back of his neck, abashed. "I just meant - he's like a brother to me too, you know? So in a way that would make you like my –"

"Don't," Shell surged abruptly to the edge of her seat. "Don't you dare make that comparison. We're *nothing* like brother and sister. Alright?"

Lee held up both hands in supplication. "You're right, you're right. I'm sorry."

After an awkward moment of silence, Shell sank back into her chair, careful to not lean too far back. Lee straightened himself up.

"I know you've probably heard awful things about me, Shell. But you have to understand - I stood by Mark no matter what. If I could go back and change how everything played out..." He faltered.

"Lee, stop," Shell's voice was as brittle as glass. "I didn't come here for what-ifs. I'm here to ask you some questions. So let's just get this over with, okay?"

"Okay," Lee scrubbed a hand down his face. "Okay. What do you want to know?"

Shell regarded him wordlessly. When she spoke again her tone was gentler.

"I'm sorry, Lee. But there's something you need to know first."

Dread crept into Lee's expression. Shell pressed on.

"I need you to stay calm when I tell you. Because I'm not leaving until I have the full story." She took a bracing breath.

"I'm really sorry, Lee, but...Mark passed away last year."

A suspended moment.

Lee unexpectedly jolted to his feet. A low, wounded noise tore from his throat as he staggered to the nearest wall. His shoulders heaved with the force of his sobs.

Shell swiped roughly at the tears now coursing down her own cheeks.

"Lee. Lee, come sit down." She crossed the room on trembling legs and guided Lee to the chair, steadying it as he collapsed into it. Lee's face crumpled in anguish.

Shell perched opposite him on the bed. She clasped his shoulder in comfort as his cries gradually tapered off into hitched breaths and sniffles.

"I know," she soothed, voice cracking. "I know."

After some time, Lee scrubbed the lingering wetness from his face. He glanced at Shell with red-rimmed eyes.

"What happened?" he rasped.

"He got sick. It all happened so fast," Shell worried her bottom lip between her teeth. "The autopsy said it was idiopathic pulmonary fibrosis."

Lee's brow furrowed in confusion. "What the fuck is that?"

"It's something to do with the lungs. We hardly understood it ourselves. One day he was fine and the next..." Shell trailed off with a helpless shrug. "He was sick for a couple of months and he died a week after his birthday."

"I can't believe it." Lee's voice was faint.

"I know," Shell's tone mirrored his own. "It wasn't like him to be ill. To go out like that. That wasn't Mark. He was invincible."

They sat in silence for a long moment, paralyzed by shared grief. Finally Shell roused herself.

"Are you alright?" she asked gently.

Lee huffed out a bleak laugh. "I can't remember the last time someone asked me that."

Regret flashed across Shell's face, but her tone remained resolved. "I really do need to ask my questions now."

Lee nodded. "I know. Just...give me a minute."

He lumbered to his feet and shuffled toward the bathroom, shoulders bowed under the weight of Shell's revelation.

Lee washed his hands in the dingy bathroom sink, the cold tap spat out a pale brown coloured liquid accompanied by a rancid odour akin to the local sewers. Turning the squeaky tap off with some difficulty, he patted his face and hands dry with a bath towel. Moments later, Lee walked towards the closed bathroom door with a new found determination in his step.

Meanwhile, Shell leaned back on the lumpy mattress in an attempt to sneak a peek at the contents of the old gym bags beside her. Before she could glimpse anything of interest, the bathroom door creaked open and Lee entered. Shell sat up straight, grabbing her handbag protectively as Lee walked over and sat down into the threadbare armchair in the centre of the room. An awkward silence permeated the space as the pair eyed each other warily.

Finally, Lee broke the tense quiet. "Okay, I'm ready," he stated, a hint of resignation in his raspy voice. "Let's do this. What do you wanna know?"

Shell placed her handbag down next to Lee's gym bags and leaned forward eagerly, perched on the very edge of the bed. The ancient springs creaked and groaned under even her slight weight.

"I want to know everything..." she began, her voice low but firm. "Everything about you and Mark."

Lee shifted uncomfortably in the chair, the faded fabric scratchy against his skin. He knew Shell wouldn't be satisfied until she had picked his brain completely clean.

"How you met, who else was involved, where you traveled to, what was planned, why it happened," Shell continued, her piercing eyes boring into Lee's. "Everything."

At that moment, a Ford Mondeo's headlights cut through the car park outside The Puppet Master Hotel. As the car slowly approached the Volvo and Fiesta, its lights switched off abruptly.

3

The air in the YMCA was musty, heavy with the scent of countless meals and years of use. It was there in the canteen, amidst the worn wooden tables and aged chairs, that Lee Barker first encountered Mark Kingham.

Lee noticed an aura of confidence around Mark, a casual charisma that drew people in.

Mark's easy smile and effortless charm made it easy for him to weave his way into the lives of those around him, and Lee was no exception.

After finishing his meal in the canteen, a sorrowful plate of beans on toast, Lee went outside and sat alone on a bench. This was something Lee had become accustomed to, almost in a ritualistic way.

The midday sun cast a warm glow over the courtyard, where people moved about in the hustle and bustle of daily life. Lee's gaze fixed on the ground as he pondered his solitary existence once more. A figure approached, catching his attention. It was Mark.

The charismatic man's vintage-inspired leather ensemble had been thoroughly scrubbed and conditioned to look as good as new. His piercing blue eyes flashed a friendly smile as he sat next to Lee. The stench of cheap aftershave washed over Lee, who tried his best to ignore it.

"Beautiful day, isn't it?" Mark said, breaking the silence.

Lee looked up to his left, his eyes meeting Mark's gaze. A hint of scepticism lingered in his expression, but he couldn't deny the genuine warmth radiating from his newfound acquaintance.

"Yeah, it is." Lee replied cautiously, unsure of where this conversation would lead.

Mark leaned back comfortably, crossing his legs. "Anyway, nice to meet you. My name's Mark Kingham. That's Kingham, not 'Kingdom'. People always get that wrong. What's your name, mate?"

"Lee."

"Lee what?"

"Oh, Lee Barker."

"Barker? Like a dog? Ruff-ruff-ruff!" Mark bellowed out, followed by a hearty laugh.

Lee was taken aback, but quickly responded to the humorous gesture with a forced giggle.

"Nah, I'm only messing, mate. How come you ended up in here anyway? What's the deal?"

This question had tugged on an old memory Lee had almost forgotten. "Well, I was homeless a few years ago."

"Oh shit, really? Sorry to hear that, mate." Mark's tone had shifted to a much more concerning one. "That's heavy that. I know how rough it is not having your own home, it's horrible isn't it?"

Lee didn't respond.

"You know, I've been through the shitter myself far too many times, more than I care to admit," Mark pulled out a small tin from his jacket's inside pocket and gestured to Lee. "Do you smoke?"

Lee nodded. Mark opened the tin and retrieved a cigarette lighter and two pre-made rollies from within. Lee watched with intrigue as Mark lit both rollies at the same time with ease, almost like a well choreographed routine that demanded admiration.

As the two men inhaled their first take of tobacco smoke, Lee was fully captivated by Mark's ability to convey emotion and vulnerability in such a short space of time.

"I'll be honest, Lee. I've not long got out of prison. Me and my mates are all here together. We've been given a second chance at life - well that's what we were told anyway. Do you believe in second chances, Lee?"

Lee exhaled a small puff of smoke after removing the rollie from his lips. "I do, yeah."

"You see, this is why I can already tell you're a great guy, Lee. You get it. You're not a judgemental prick like the rest of them out there. You know how the real world works."

Mark's voice carried an underlying strength that resonated with Lee's own yearning for connection and friendship.

"People like us, we always had to graft the hard way," Mark's passion was seeping through his vocabulary. "Nothing was ever handed down to us, no silver spoon, no help from anyone, we did it all ourselves and got on with it. And look where it got us. Here. The fucking YMCA."

Lee couldn't remember the last time he had felt so understood and accepted.

"Guys like you and me, we were left to fend for ourselves. The world we live in no longer accepts us, no matter how hard we work. It's all bollocks. The lies, the false promises, the corruption, all of it."

The weight of Lee's loneliness seemed to dissipate with each passing moment in Mark's presence.

"That's why we need to stick together, Lee. We're a dying breed. This world will continue to eat us up and shit us out unless we put a stop to it ourselves. Don't you agree?"

"Of course I agree." Lee responded.

"I can also tell that nobody else in this shithole gives a fuck about you. Am I right?"

Lee hesitated. "I guess so."

"I knew it. I've seen you a few times out here and you're always on your own. I don't get it though.

Why would anyone overlook you?" Mark shifted himself slightly closer towards Lee.

"You're a nice guy, Lee. You don't deserve to be treated like an afterthought, especially in a place like this where the rest of the world already looks at us like that."

Lee found solace in Mark's words, the honesty behind them being too obvious to ignore. He also found a sense of belonging that transcended their differing backgrounds.

"I promise you now, Lee. Me and my mates, we'll look after you. We've got your back."

Lee could no longer contain the smile that had already been forming for quite some time. "Thank you Mark."

Mark returned the smile with one of his own. "Don't mention it."

"Sorry if I misheard, but before, did you say your mates from prison are also in here with us, yeah?" Lee asked.

"Yeah, they're over there. Would you like to meet them?"

The urgency in Mark's question took Lee by surprise. "Er - yeah, sure."

Lee's eyes quickly scanned the courtyard, trying to spot anyone who could potentially be associated with Mark, but the dozens of people spread out within the vicinity was too much for Lee to designate a single candidate.

Mark stood up and dropped his rollie to the ground below, pressing the sole of his cherry blossom-cleansed size nine on top of the lit tubed tobacco, diminishing its burn.

Despite the courtyard buzzing with activity, Mark's whistle pierced through the air like a bird calling out for its infants to return home.

Within a matter of seconds, Lee found himself stood up, locking eyes with Mark's friends from prison.

Lee watched in awe as they moved towards him from across the courtyard with a certain swagger, their tattoos peeking out from beneath their sleeves, a testament to their shared experiences.

As Lee came face to face with them, he continued to observe them. Mark's friends introduced themselves one by one. Their personalities shone through in every interaction.

Freddie Taylor, a striking man with strawberry blonde hair, exuded confidence and intelligence.

He possessed an air of mystery that piqued Lee's curiosity. He couldn't help but wonder what secrets lay beneath his composed exterior.

Sean Hole stood tall and imposing, his muscular frame intimidating just by its mere presence. His hot temper was evident in the way his fists clenched and unclenched, ready for action at a moment's notice. It was clear that Sean thrived on instilling fear in others, relishing the chaos that followed in his wake.

Karl Roberts, in contrast, radiated warmth and kindness. His gentle mannerisms seemed out of place among the hardened former prison inmates. Lee couldn't help but feel a sense of calmness from him.

And then there was Paul Knight, an enigma whose presence sent chills down Lee's spine. His silent nature added to Lee's difficulty to gauge his true intentions or loyalties. Paul had an unwavering dedication towards Mark that both intrigued and unsettled Lee.

Later that evening, the air was thick with tension as Lee, Mark and his friends gathered in the dimly lit bike shed next to the courtyard.

Lee stood at the perimeter, his heart pounding in his chest as he observed the flickering fluorescent lights casting eerie shadows across the shed, amplifying the sense of foreboding.

Mark's friendly nature was helping Lee to settle his nerves. "His name's Peter. We met him here a couple of days ago. He's just what we're looking for."

At that moment, the door to the bike shed opened slowly. Lee, Mark, Freddie, Sean, Karl and Paul focused their attention on Peter as he entered the tiny space, being careful to shut the door quietly after him.

Peter had a toned physique, clearly a gym rat in his spare time. His height wasn't as complementary to his frame as he would've liked it to have been, but no doubt he was an imposing force to be reckoned with.

After pleasantries were exchanged, Mark introduced Lee to Peter. "So this is Lee. He's never been to prison either, plus he only just passed his driving test a few weeks ago, so that's perfect. He doesn't want to get involved in the business side of things, but he's a good lad. You'll get on well with him." Peter nodded his head approvingly.

Mark's attention switched to Lee. "And with Peter having no criminal record too, that helps us out, big time. But yeah, that's pretty much it."

Lee and Peter smiled at each other and shook hands briefly. Lee could tell that Peter was probably just as shy or as uncomfortable as he was. He was another lonely soul who just wanted to be accepted and feel important. Lee knew he could trust Peter.

Mark leaned back, his eyes alight with a mischievous gleam. "You see, Lee," he continued, his voice barely audible above the silence. "We have the chance to live a life others can only dream of. The money, the freedom, it's all within our reach."

Lee watched intently, drawn to Mark's charm and magnetism. The thought of financial stability and a future free from loneliness swirled his mind. "But what about the obvious risks?" he asked cautiously, his eyes searching Mark's face for reassurance. "That's all I'm worried about, to be honest."

A knowing smile played on Mark's lips as he leaned closer, his ocean blue eyes glittering with adventure. "Yes, of course there are risks," he admitted, his tone laced with boyish excitement. "But think about the rewards, Lee. The thrill of outsmarting everyone, the power that comes with being at the top of the food chain for once. We'll be untouchable."

Lee's face screamed trepidation.

"Besides, we only need you to drive us for now. It's up to you what you want to do in the future, but this is all we need from you right now. We just need to get things started first."

Mark draped his arm over Lee's shoulder as he directed his attention towards everyone else in the bike shed, one by one.

"Sean and Peter will provide the muscle, Paul is responsible for checking if the stock is legit, Freddie's gonna arrange all the deals and Karl is handling all the technical aspects. I'll be the salesman and you'll be the driver. That's all you need to focus on. So please, don't worry yourself, okay? We're all in this together, I promise."

Lee felt everyone's gaze weigh heavily on him. As he took one last look round and saw the determination in these men's faces, Lee knew he had no choice. Despite the internal panic of potentially getting in trouble with the law, deep down he agreed with Mark's plan. "Okay. I'm in."

Mark's allure was undeniable. He had successfully wrapped Lee in a cloak of camaraderie, blurring the lines between right and wrong, loyalty and self-preservation.

Several weeks later, Mark's gang had begun to set the wheels in motion for the illegal activities they were going to get involved in - the main one being drug dealing.

Peter, however, didn't last very long with the gang, much to Lee's dismay. Peter subsequently 'chickened out' and decided to pursue an honest living. His presence wasn't missed by everyone else.

Money wasn't Lee's primary motivation, but during the initial six months of working for Mark, he was paid a generous sum of five hundred pounds per day.

They were driving together five, six, or even seven days a week at that time. As Mark's earnings increased, he started paying Lee a thousand pounds per day.

Lee wasn't one to splurge on extravagant things, only spending money on necessities. Consequently, he saved a significant amount - a few grand short of a million pounds.

For almost seven years, every deal went smoothly without any major issues, except for Lee's last one, which was in Tottenham.

4

As Lee's story unfolded, Shell's body language grew tense and rigid. Her eyebrows knitted together in concentration as she listened.

Lee explained to Shell that whenever just himself and Mark drove to the location of a deal, they had a strict routine. Lee had to drop Mark off, drive around aimlessly for exactly ten minutes and then return to pick him up.

Without fail, Mark would always appear at the same time. This precise timing was crucial for every transaction and any deviation would result in the deal being cancelled.

However, on that particular day in Tottenham, Mark was already present and visibly perspiring when Lee returned.

During the drive home, Lee sensed that Mark was on edge. The car was heavy with tension as Lee and Mark kept their eyes focused on the road ahead, not once turning to check to see if the other was looking at them.

The air seemed to thicken with unspoken words, the two of them locked in a silent battle of wills.

Lee's voice trembled slightly as he spoke, his tone laced with a mix of concern and accusation. "Mark, something doesn't feel right, you're acting a bit weird. Is everything alright?"

Mark's face contorted momentarily with a flicker of defensiveness before settling into an expression of feigned innocence. He leaned forward in his seat, his voice calm yet tinged with an icy edge. "Lee, I said I'm fine. It was just hot in there and I'm getting tired now. Just drop it."

Lee hesitated for a moment, his mind swimming with conflicting emotions. He had always trusted Mark implicitly, but something wasn't adding up. Lee could feel it in his bones.

Summoning his courage, Lee glanced towards Mark and pressed on, his voice firm yet filled with vulnerability. "I don't know, there's something about that deal. I feel like we're being set up or something."

Mark's mask slipped for a brief instant, his eyes narrowing as if caught off guard by Lee's astuteness. But just as quickly, he composed himself, leaning back to meet Lee's gaze directly. "You're being paranoid," he retorted sharply. "I don't know what else to tell you, Lee."

"You would tell me if there's something I need to know, right?"

"There's nothing you or the others need to worry about, okay? Everything is fine, I promise. Now let's change the subject."

And with that, Lee could only take Mark's word for it. He knew if he continued to press him any further, an argument would ensue.

Shell interrupted Lee. "Sorry to cut you off, but by any chance, when Mark said 'the others' did he mean his mates you met in the YMCA?"

"I think so, yeah, why?" Lee asked.

"Did you or Mark - or anyone else - ever come across someone called Robbie?" Shell's question hinted she had some personal interest in whoever this Robbie was.

Lee cocked his head back, looking towards the ceiling, lost in thought. "Robbie...Robbie... I think it might ring a bell. What's his surname?"

"No one knows his surname. Big stocky guy, black hair, beard, smells like cigars."

Lee continued to sift through his memories. "We might've met someone like that at one point, but not too sure. Why, who is he?"

Shell stamped down her authority. "It doesn't matter. I'm the one asking the questions."

"Yeah, you're right. Sorry."

Before Lee's account went on, Shell stood up and began pacing the small hotel room, her body coiled tight like a snake ready to strike.

"Is there anything else you need to tell me before I address the elephant in the room?" Shell's eyes focused on the gym bags on Lee's bed.

Lee stumbled on his words as he looked around the room. "Er - well, after that day, I started to get doubts over our safety. Mark wasn't himself after that and it started to rub off on the rest of us."

Shell stood directly behind Lee. "Doubts over your safety?"

"Yeah."

"Okay," Shell walked over to the bed and gestured towards the gym bags. "So what do you have in these?"

"One's full of money and the other is my personal stuff, like clothes and that."

"Mind if I take a look?"

Lee considered this momentarily, but didn't want to come across more secretive than he already had. "Yeah, sure."

Shell grabbed the gym bag closest to her handbag at the edge of the bed and fully unzipped it, revealing multiple stacks of folded money. There was easily over a quarter of a million pounds stuffed in there, possibly more.

After silently admiring the amount of cash she was looking down at, Shell zipped the bag back up and opened up the other one.

Inside the second bag was a small pile of scrunched up clothes, a few bottles of water, cutlery, a makeshift First Aid kit, toiletries and a few plastic bags containing ready made sandwiches and snacks. Lee was telling the truth.

But there was something that caught Shell's eye. Something which slightly raised her concern.

A steak knife. Sharp enough to be used as a deadly weapon if needed. Lee could have already used it as part of his cutlery set, but the cleanliness of the cold hard steel said otherwise.

This was Lee's last line of defence.

Playing it off like she hadn't noticed it, Shell decided she needed to try and retrieve the knife from Lee's possessions while she had the chance to do so. She had to keep it cool though.

"I'll be honest, Lee. There's no way I could stretch out this amount of money on shit hotels, rented cars and meal deals for two years."

Lee looked slightly embarrassed. "I'm used to it. Could you pass me a bottle of water, please?"

An opportunity. Shell had to think fast. "Yeah sure, can I have one as well?"

Lee nodded. Shell picked up a bottle from inside the bag and lightly threw it towards Lee, but at an angle where she knew he would fail to catch it.

The bottle fell onto the floor in front of the bed. "Sorry about that." Shell's apology seemed convincing enough.

"It's alright." Lee bent forward in the chair, his arm outstretched trying to reach the bottle.

Shell grabbed the steak knife and a bottle of water for herself. She very quickly placed the knife underneath her handbag just in time as Lee sat back up in his chair, bottle in hand.

Raising her own bottle of water in appreciation of his kindness, Shell caught Lee's attention. "Thank you. I'll save it for later."

"You're welcome." Lee opened his bottle and leant his head back as he drank a couple of much needed gulps of water.

With one hand, Shell simultaneously picked up her handbag and the steak knife, still concealed underneath, hiding the weapon from Lee's line of vision.

Opening up the bag while walking past Lee, Shell put the bottle of water and steak knife inside her handbag, clandestinely.

Unaware of what Shell had just done, Lee closed the lid and put the bottle on his bed. He then turned the chair around to face Shell, who now stood near the window, holding onto her closed handbag.

"So you said you had doubts over your safety, yeah?" Shell asked, picking up where Lee left off.

"Yeah," Lee replied, with a slight tone of cowardice. "Everyone's behaviour was starting to get a bit too much for me. I really don't like confrontations, I'm not good at them."

Lee continued. "A few weeks after what happened in Tottenham, I spoke to Mark in private one day and asked him if it would be okay if I didn't...participate anymore. That was the best way I could put it to him."

Lee paused briefly. "I told him I'll always be his friend, but it was getting too much. I already had enough money to live off for the rest of my life, so what was the point?"

After slightly leaning back in the chair, Lee briefly glanced up at the ceiling before looking towards Shell. The shift in his body language was enough to put Shell on alert.

"Also, a little part of me thought it was coming to an end anyway, so I thought it was best that I got out before anything bad could happen." Lee's voice was sounding different somehow, almost as if he was still holding onto a part of himself he had not yet revealed to Shell.

"To Mark's credit, he completely understood. He apologised that I felt that way and he let me go. But right before I left, I gave him a present."

Lee lightly placed his hand over the zipped pocket on his trousers, where he had placed the gold ring.

"United Kingham...he had that tattooed on his arm and I knew he loved jewellery. It was the perfect gift for him."

Shell watched in complete silence, observing how Lee had cracked a wry smile that also came across slightly callous.

"He gave me a hug and told me that we'd see each other again soon. He wanted me to get a passport sorted so we could go on holiday together at some point."

Lee suddenly lost all shred of positive nostalgia. "That was the last time I ever..." Lee stopped himself from finishing his train of thought.

Shell took it upon herself to interject before Lee succumbed to his grief. "How long after what happened in Tottenham did you speak to Mark about quitting?"

Shell's question had brought Lee back from the brink of another teary eyed episode. "Er - a few weeks. Maybe three?"

"Right, okay. You know what my next question is gonna be." Shell's statement carried a significant amount of weight to it, a level of understanding she was hoping Lee would pick up on.

Lee knew he had reached the main question Shell wanted answering all evening. "What happened the day after I quit?"

"Bingo."

Finally, Shell understood that Lee was on the same level as her. This was the moment of truth she had been longing for.

Lee stood up, stretched his legs and took a few deep breaths.

Shell clutched her handbag as she felt the tension in the room switch, almost as if she now feared what Lee was about to do or say next.

5

Lee perched tensely on the edge of his creaky bed, absently staring at the cracked and peeling walls of his modest flat in Southport.

The decision to walk away from Mark's gang after almost seven years, only the day before having felt like the best thing for Lee, now seemed like it was the worst thing he had ever done.

Lee knew he had to move forward and embrace a new life without seeing his best friends every day. The constant question of 'Did I make the right decision?' was ever so present in his mind.

At that moment, his phone on the nightstand lit up with a notification. Lee stood up and walked over to retrieve it.

The day was Saturday. The time was 17:04. The phone battery was 100% fully charged.

An unwanted weather update.

Lee chose to ignore it by closing the screen on his phone, but suddenly something else came through at that second. An incoming call from Freddie Taylor.

Lee almost couldn't believe it. Why was Freddie calling him at this time? Mark had already discussed the details with Lee about the deal in Manchester and how it was due to take place on that day at five o'clock in the evening. This was not the right time to make a phone call.

After answering the call, Lee put the phone on speaker mode. Before he could even muster up a timid greeting, Freddie's animated voice stopped him from doing so.

"You fucking dirty rat!" Freddie shouted down the phone. "You set us all up, you horrible cunt! I'm gonna fucking kill you!"

Lee's mind raced as Freddie's angry accusations continued to ring out of the tiny speaker.

"That's why you quit yesterday wasn't it? You told the bizzies about our warehouse in Manchester! You had it all planned out!"

Lee placed the phone down on the nightstand and promptly sat back down on his bed to rub his palms on his jeans. His heart was pounding with adrenaline and dread.

"What are you talking about?" Lee asked desperately, mouth dry. "I haven't said anything to the police, I swear!" His leg bounced anxiously as Freddie spat insults and threats through the phone.

"Mark trusted you! How could you do this to us?" Freddie implored. He sounded out of breath, like he was being chased down while trying to seek shelter.

Lee's palms grew sweaty as he struggled to stay calm. "Freddie, I don't know what you're talking about! What happened? What's going on?"

"Don't fucking play dumb with me you little rat! There's a whole fucking firing squad here, eye in the sky, the whole nine yards! Everyone's getting arrested as we speak! Mark, Sean, all of us!"

Lee knew everyone else would readily believe these accusations of betrayal and come seeking vengeance. "Freddie, listen! I swear--"

"Shut the fuck up!" Freddie growled back menacingly. "We trusted you and this is how you repaid us! When we get out of this, we're all coming for you, Lee! You're fucking dead!"

The call disconnected abruptly, leaving Lee reeling in a state of numbness.

The reality of Lee's situation came crashing down. His life was now in serious jeopardy. There was only one thing on his mind.

Lee had to disappear completely.

With shaking hands, Lee hastily threw all of his money and clothes into two gym bags, leaving no trace of his presence in the flat. He also ditched his phone, knowing it would be tracked by not just Mark, but also by the police.

Shouldering his gym bags, Lee took one last look at the first real home he'd known since leaving the YMCA, sadness welling within him. But it was no longer safe here.

Lee stepped out into the night, pulse racing as he constantly glanced over his shoulder. He wasn't the best at exercise, but on this night, he managed to squeeze every last ounce of energy he had in his body in order to maintain a brisk stroll without losing its pace.

Lee made his way to the train station, hyper aware of every passerby. Paranoia gnawed at him, certain he was being watched. Knowing he couldn't stay anywhere for too long, he drilled into his head that he had to remain an elusive ghost from that moment on.

Later that evening, after arriving at a small hotel in Formby, Lee got a room for the night and collapsed onto the bed, completely exhausted, both physically and mentally.

Sleep evaded him once more. His mind was spinning with fear about what tomorrow would bring. Lee longed desperately for any friendly face, but the shadows of his past ensured he could trust no one.

Lee eventually closed his eyes after going back and forth in his mind over how long he planned to live like this.

As long as he had the money and he could change his physical appearance as much as humanly possible, Lee would commit to living on the run.

No family. No friends. No stable home. A life that Lee was unfavourably suited for prior to meeting Mark Kingham that day in the YMCA.

This time he wasn't seeking a life of companionship, he was avoiding it at all cost.

6

When Lee finished the telling of his saga, an uneasy quiet settled between himself and Shell once again.

Lee's eyes were moist with emotion from dredging up the tumultuous memories. Shell remained stone-faced, but her aggressive pacing had ceased.

"Are you hungry? I could do with some food after all that, don't know about you." An apparent gesture of goodwill from Shell.

"Er - yeah, okay." Lee said, confused.

Shell put her handbag down on the floor where she was standing and walked over to the gym bag with the food bags inside, grabbing them and passing one to Lee, which he took.

Shell and Lee both removed a sandwich and a packet of crisps each from their bags. Lee sat back down on the chair after grabbing his bottle of water off the bed, whereas Shell sat down on the floor, opposite the chair, cross legged. She then placed her food down in front of her, next to her handbag. Lee balanced his food and drink on his lap.

"First of all, thanks for all of that," Shell started. "I'm sorry I've come across the way I have, but you have to understand, this has been two years in the making. Nobody could get a hold of you, you just vanished."

Lee expressed his understanding with a simple few nods.

"But also, I know you've had it rough too," Shell's sincerity allowed her the time to carefully consider her next approach. "Finding out about Mark's death this way was the last thing you needed and I'm sorry about that. I know he was a stubborn bastard sometimes, but I could tell how much he cared about you. I understand you're still processing all of this."

Lee didn't want to be reminded of Mark's death. He hastefully changed the subject. "What actually happened after everyone got arrested?"

Slightly startled with Lee's abruptness, Shell gathered her thoughts and decided to respond here on out with the same abrasiveness she had shown him up until that point.

"Am I alright to know what happened, yeah?" Lee asked tentatively.

"I suppose it's only fair." Shell's response was layered with undertones of sarcasm that disguised itself in politeness.

After taking a bite of her sandwich, Shell looked Lee dead in the eye. This was now her opportunity to be in the driver's seat. She was going to savour every word she dished out.

"After Mark got arrested, my dad's house got searched and that's what pissed us off the most, because Mark kept me and my dad out of it all. We never got a penny from him because he said he couldn't put us at risk like that."

Lee took a bite of his sandwich, listening with intent.

"We were getting harassed by everyone all the time, so to prove our innocence, I kept visiting Mark in prison so he could give me the names of every person he ever worked with, proving it would rule me and my dad out. He gave me everybody's name."

Lee began to feel indisposed.

"Sean, Paul, Freddie, Karl, every dealer he did business with, literally everybody, except yours."

Shell continued to stare deep into Lee's eyes, sensing the abyss that consumed him. "For whatever reason, Mark was adamant that his driver wasn't worth mentioning."

Each bite that Lee took of his sandwich was forced. The chewing became methodical. Swallowing turned into a chore.

Shell persisted. "Mark also put the word out to everyone not to grass on his driver, which only made things worse, because I wasn't allowed to visit any of the other guys anyway."

Another attempt to ingest food. Lee now struggled to even open his mouth.

"Lee, you have to understand, this is what made me and my dad more suspicious of you."

Shell broke eye contact at that moment, which said an awful lot about her disdain with the entire situation. "We got fed up with Mark not telling us anything, so my dad got in touch with his mates that track people down for a living. I told Mark about it and that's when he told me he knew he was set up by someone."

The undercurrent of tension still crackled dangerously beneath the surface. The suspicion still glimmered in Shell's eyes each time she looked back at Lee.

"Mark was in the middle of figuring out who it was when he got sick. After that, everything changed. The last time I saw him, he gave me that gold ring and said your name for the first time. I don't know if he knew he was dying, but he finally put my mind at ease when he told me."

Lee was unsure how to respond, or whether he should respond at all.

"I was going through a lot at that time, right before Mark died," Shell bowed her head. "I was just glad that my dad finally had a name to go off, but even having your name wasn't enough. You'd been living off the grid for most of your life, there's not a lot of official government documents about you, and your driver's licence photo was taken when you were in your late twenties when you looked completely different."

Shell lifted her head slowly to reach Lee's concerned gaze. "On top of all that, the guy I started getting serious with turned out to be an abusive twat...and then Mark died."

Trying to distract herself from getting too emotional, Shell placed all of her food down onto the floor away from her, apparently having also lost her appetite.

"That was it for me. Things had to change, I couldn't carry on like that anymore, I couldn't. I was biding my time to get out of the toxic relationship I was in and I started working closer with my dad." Shell paused, this particular mention of her dad had brought a certain memory to the forefront of her mind.

"My dad, bless him, his whole purpose in life after burying his only son is finding out who set him up...and tracking *you* down, that's it. Nothing else matters to him now, not even me."

Lee expressed genuine sorrow towards Shell, wanting to say something to her, but no words came to mind.

"Karl Roberts got three years, but he might be out now. Sean Hole got five, Paul Knight and Freddie Taylor each got seven. Mark got ten years, only did eleven months." The decibel in Shell's voice dropped at the insinuation of Mark's premature demise. "And in case you're wondering, you probably would've got two or three years at the most."

Lee finally mustered up the courage to respond. "Feels like I have done my time."

"You know, it's always baffled me how Mark thought you were innocent and why the police never bothered looking for you either."

"What do you mean?" Lee asked, faint-heartedly.

"Come on, Lee, I wasn't born yesterday. How is it that you were the only one that got out unscathed?"

Shell's friendly facade had now fully slipped away as glaring holes in Lee's story left her convinced he wasn't being completely transparent as promised.

"Me and my dad never got a penny from Mark and we've been accused of all sorts by the police, but yet you worked for him for nearly ten years, had all this inside knowledge, got paid a million quid for being his taxi driver and not one brainless bobby out there has ever reached out to you with an arrest!"

Lee retaliated by standing on his feet. His sandwich and open packet of crisps spilled all over the floor. "I don't know, Shell!"

Shell responded by also standing up, figuratively and literally. "Don't lie to me! There's something not right about this!"

"I've told you the truth!"

"Bollocks!"

"I have!"

"Then why were you let off? Why?"

"I don't know, I honestly don't know!"

Shell tried her best to remain calm and composed. She continued to speak from this moment on in a quiet tone. However, Shell noticed the obvious look of guilt on Lee's face.

"Lee, I believe everything you've told me about how you met Mark and the other guys, how you worked together for as long as you did and the fact that you were just his driver. I believe all of that because Mark told me the exact same thing."

Lee nervously gulped the saliva in his mouth as Shell continued.

"What I don't believe is everything you said about the deal in Tottenham three weeks before you asked Mark to quit. How you approached him the day before they all got arrested, and how you found out about the raid. I don't believe any of that."

Lee felt the colour in his face drain.

"Mark gave me that ring the very last time I saw him. I remember every single word he said to me that day. I've been replaying it over and over in my head. I can still vividly recall every word he said, how he said it, the heavy breaths he'd take between sentences..."

Shell had said to her dad, Michael, that she was going to have a word with Mark, at his request. Visiting hours in a prison hospital were notoriously strict with their rules. Only one family member at a time.

Michael stayed put in the waiting room, wondering what Mark wanted to say to Shell.

As Shell stepped into Mark's room, the prison guard reminded her that she had five minutes. "Yes, I know. Thanks." She closed the door behind her after the unpleasant guard had vacated the room.

Approaching Mark's bed, surrounded by blinking machines, see-through tubes, and more wires and cables than the eye could see, Shell cracked both sides of her mouth with an obligatory smile. "So what's up? We've gotta leave soon."

"I know, I know. Come here." Mark held out his palm, the gold ring resting in the centre. It glinted in the low light as he offered it to Shell.

Shell walked round the bed and stood close to Mark's side, quizzically observing what was in her brother's hand.

"Take it," Mark said, his voice barely above a whisper. He gently took Shell's hand and turned it over, placing the ring in her open palm and curling her fingers closed over it. "It's a 'thank you' gift from my driver...Lee Barker."

"Fuck off!" Shell's eyes widened, a smile spreading across her face as she inspected the ring, turning it over between her fingers.

Shell made to call out to their dad in the waiting room, to share the good news of finally having the name of the mystery driver, but Mark shook his head sharply.

"Don't tell dad yet," Mark cautioned, grasping Shell's wrist lightly to stop her. "I need to tell you something."

Shell paused, a smile fading as she noted the grave tone in her brother's voice. Mark drew in a deep breath, his shoulders sagging as if weighted down by some invisible burden. When he continued, his words were slow and measured.

"Shell...I *know* Lee. If you ever meet him, you'll see for yourself that he's not the brightest bulb." Mark's voice caught, thick with emotion. Shell listened with growing unease.

"But I know you and dad are more stubborn than me so I'll tell you this. Just promise you'll go easy on Lee, okay? It's probably nothing."

Mark inhaled sharply, blinking back the tears that sprang unbidden to his eyes.

"I did a deal in Tottenham a few weeks before the raid happened. Lee was late picking me up at the drop off point, which was unusual for him. It was the one and only time he was ever late picking me up. He never said why, but I didn't ask him."

Shell knew that she was listening to vital information that shouldn't be forgotten.

"He was sweating and he didn't talk much after that. I pulled him to one side and said we were gonna do one last deal." Mark trailed off with a shuddering sigh, followed by a painful intake of oxygen, scrubbing a hand over his face to shield the pain from his sister's watchful eye.

After a long moment, Mark met Shell's worried gaze once more.

"A few weeks later he gave me that ring and said he just wanted to go home, so I let him go. I think it was just the lifestyle, he'd had enough and wanted out. I don't blame him."

Mark took another sharp breath. "Honestly, by that point, we were all out."

Shell mutely nodded, closing her fist around the ring, still warm from her brother's touch.

"I know I was set up, Shell, but trust me, it wasn't Lee. He had fuck all to do with it. Wrong place, wrong time...I know it."

Lee froze like a cornered animal as he watched tears slip down Shell's cheeks, visually reliving the pain her dying brother was in.

Overwhelmed and panicked by his fabric of lies crashing down around him, Lee quickly retreated to the dingy bathroom once again.

"No! Lee! Stop!" Shell hurriedly followed after Lee, but her words fell on deaf ears.

"Leave me alone!" The reverberating slam of the flimsy hollow door punctuated Lee's desperate shout.

"Lee, open the door!" Shell pleaded.

Lee's muffled sobs echoed from the other side, the too-bright fluorescent light seeping into the darkened bedroom through the cracks.

After a couple of failed attempts to open the bathroom door, Shell stood back and rested her head against the wall behind her, wiping her tears away.

The original question that plagued Shell's mind for over a year suddenly came right back to the forefront. Was Lee going to tell her the truth?

7

Lee sat slumped on the cold tile floor, back pressed against the bathroom door as he wiped away the tears streaming down his cheeks. He choked back sobs, trying in vain to stem the overwhelming emotion.

"Just go away." Lee uttered faintly, voice ragged.

Shell exhaled slowly, gaze flitting upwards a moment as she stood supporting her stance against the wall. Her tone softened marginally as she focused on the closed door. "You know I can't go away, Lee. Not yet. You lied to me."

Lee's crying eased, leaving his face blotchy and eyes puffy. But no words came to his defense. Trapped by Shell's accusations and his own lies, the loose splinters of the door digging into his back served as a physical reminder of his powerlessness in that moment.

"Should have been honest from the start," Shell continued, a brittle edge to her words.

"I warned you it would only make things worse. How can I believe anything you say now? You told me it was *Mark* who was acting weird in Tottenham!"

A flare of anger kindled in Lee's gut as Shell's recriminations washed over him. "Why didn't you tell me what Mark said when you got here? Why'd you make me go through all that? There was no need." His voice climbed in agitation.

Shell straightened, posture rigid. "Are you blaming this on me? Don't you dare–"

"FUCKING LISTEN TO ME!" Lee exploded, slamming his fist against the hollow door in emphasis. He surged to his feet, years of pent-up hurt and frustration erupting to the surface.

"You're calling me a liar?" Lee bellowed out. "You turn up tonight telling me my best friend died last year and then you immediately asked me questions about shit that happened years ago, expecting me to remember every fucking little bit of detail!"

Lee's chest heaved between rapid breaths. "All the while I'm still trying to process that the one person in my entire fucking life who actually cared about me is now dead!"

Shell recoiled slightly in the wake of his tirade, eyes dropping to study the carpet.

Lee was just revving up, the gates fully open. "And you, you sat there eating *my* food, forcing me to play your own little game, already knowing every answer to every fucking question you were gonna ask me!"

Shell had no choice but to stand there and allow Lee to continue without interruption.

"Didn't give a flying fuck about my feelings, just 'nah mate, here's the worst news you'll ever hear, but enough of that, come on, you need to tell me what size shoe I am - even though I already know - and if you don't get it right, you're a fucking liar'!"

Lee tried calming himself down by turning away from the door and closing his eyes, taking slow paces in the small bathroom. Shell was motionless, still looking at the floor.

"I can't think about what happened at the end, Shell. It's too painful...I lost everything." Lee rasped, raking both hands through the small amount of hair left on his head, before resuming his frenetic pacing within the confines of the small bathroom.

"I've been lonely my entire life. Never went to school, had to do everything myself because no one wanted to be seen with me, let alone help me." Lee walked up to the bathroom mirror, staring at the reflection of somebody he used to recognise.

"By the time I was nineteen, I'd already slept under bridges, bushes and benches. It was normal for me," Lee gritted his teeth for a brief moment. "But I finally had enough of it, so I got myself set up in the YMCA, got involved with the Prince's Trust, got a job stacking shelves, took reading and writing courses. It was great."

Shell appeared to look more understanding. Lee's words were laced with pain that even she could relate to on some level.

"I met Mark a few years later and he was the first person who ever asked me if I was okay, the *first* one," Lee pushed his tongue into the side of his bottom lip, feigning a smirk. "You don't forget shit like that. When things are good, you remember it, but when it's bad, everything becomes a blur."

Shell leaned her hands against the frame of the bathroom door, taking in every word.

"Those seven years with Mark were the happiest days of my life. Fuck the money, fuck the drugs, I only cared about the six of us. We were a family." Lee finally looked away from his reflection, almost defiantly.

"Mark telling us stories, driving up and down motorways at night singing Beatles songs, laughing every time. Living in a place I called home. Being so grateful I slept under a thick duvet instead of wet leaves...laying down on a king size bed instead of slanted concrete," The pain of reliving his glory days almost prevented Lee from carrying on speaking. "I was happy."

Shell released her grip on the doorframe and straightened in anticipation.

"You can call me a liar if you want, Shell, but you've got no right playing with me like that." Lee's voice filled with conviction.

Shell wet her lips uncertainly. "You're right, Lee. I'm sorry," she offered softly. "No more questions about the past or anything I've already asked. You have my word."

Lee hesitated, part of him wanting to cling to the rage shielding his grief, but it was a heavy burden to bear alone. "You promise?"

"I promise." Shell glanced over to her handbag on the floor across the room and remembered placing her bible inside it earlier in the evening. She then turned to the bathroom door and asked, "Lee, do you believe in God?"

Lee wasn't expecting a question like that. "I do, but it's complicated. I've never been to church or anything."

Shell reassured him, saying, "That's okay. The reason I ask is because there's a passage from the bible that I live by. Luke 12:48. Have you heard of that?"

"No."

"'To whom much is given, much will be required'...It means we're held responsible for what we have. If we've been blessed, it's a no-brainer that we help others whenever we can, no matter what." Shell replied.

Silence. Shell wasn't certain if Lee had even paid attention to what she said.

"Yeah, I suppose so." Lee finally answered, in a small voice.

Shell continued. "Lee, I came here tonight in the hopes that I could find out what really happened in Tottenham and Manchester... Mark wasn't an angel, he lived a very selfish life and never settled down properly to enjoy everything he had around him, but he didn't deserve to die so young, surrounded by guards and doctors while gasping for air...He was willing to serve his time, he was happy to own up to his mistakes, but he didn't get the chance to find closure. That's why it's my responsibility now. Mark Kingham deserves to rest in peace. That's all I want. That's why I'm here."

The bathroom door unlocked, causing Shell to step back. As the door opened, her stoicism remained convincing.

8

The atmosphere was heavy with uneasy silence as Lee slowly stepped towards Shell. Her widened eyes followed his cautious approach, uncertainty clouding her expression.

"Can I give you a hug?" Lee's voice trembled as he spoke.

Shell's face registered surprise at the unexpected request. Her eyes flitted up and down, taking in Lee's slumped shoulders and downcast eyes. She paused briefly.

"Yeah, okay." Hesitation cloaked Shell's response.

Lee moved towards Shell, enveloping her slender frame in his arms. She stood rigid in the embrace, her arms hanging limply at her sides, her gaze directed away from him as she avoided returning the hug. Lee clung to her, his body beginning to shake with suppressed sobs.

"I'm really sorry." Lee choked out.

"It's alright, I know." Shell responded mechanically, her tone sounding disconnected and distracted.

After long seconds of profoundly awkward stillness, Shell carefully extracted herself from Lee's grip. She turned and walked purposefully across the cluttered floor, being careful to avoid stepping onto the crisps and half-eaten sandwiches.

Reaching down, Shell retrieved her handbag where it lay abandoned amid the mess on the floor. As she swung the bag's strap over her shoulder, Lee shuffled heavily over to perch on the edge of his messy bed.

Shell slid her Nokia phone from her trouser pocket, breaking the uneasy silence. "Oh, before I forget, I'm only gonna ask you one more question."

Lee brought his thumb across his damp eyes before raising his head. "What's that?"

Shell turned the phone over in her hands as she spoke, her eyes downcast. "Can we swap numbers?"

Lee looked taken aback. "What? Why?"

"Because there's no way I'm gonna leave here knowing you're alone every day," Shell stated firmly, empathy resonating in her tone. "No one deserves to live their life like that."

Shell raised her eyes to meet Lee's gaze. "I have a big family and the thought of not having them in my life doesn't bear thinking about."

Uncertainty clouded Lee's features once more. "You want us to be friends?"

Shell gave a small, sympathetic smile. "I mean, let's be honest, the only reason me and you have any sort of connection is because of Mark," She paused, considering her words. "However, I know he'd love it if we stayed in touch."

Lee nodded slowly, leaning down to grab his scuffed flip phone from his open gym bag. He held it limply as Shell continued.

"Is that okay, yeah?" Shell asked gently.

Lee's face became stern, his shoulders stiffening. "You aren't gonna turn me in are you?" His words held an edge of desperation.

Shell looked affronted. "What? No, of course not."

Lee stared at Shell. "You promise?"

"Yes. Why would I do that? You told me everything you remembered and you said you didn't have anything to do with Mark's arrest. So what more is there?" Shell replied firmly. "I can't keep prodding at you all night, Lee, not after what just happened. You need time to grieve and me being here right now isn't helping at all."

Shell gestured towards the door with one hand. "So we'll swap phone numbers, I'll go back to my room and we'll call it a night."

Worry creased Lee's forehead. "You're leaving?"

"Yeah, my room is just outside. Number 48. Why, what's wrong?" Shell responded with a confused tone. "Don't you want me to go?"

Lee hesitated, a pleading look entering his eyes. "Well, can't we..." His voice trailed off uncertainly.

Shell gazed at Lee questioningly. "What?"

The desperation on Lee's face intensified. "Can't we talk about something else?"

Perplexment coloured Shell's features. "Like what?"

Lee gave a half-hearted shrug, his eyes downcast once more. "I dunno, just something else."

Shell stepped towards Lee, her voice gentle. "Lee, if you want to have a chat, we can do that tomorrow, okay?"

Lee opened and closed his mouth wordlessly before choking out, "I mean, I, well-"

Gently touching Lee's arm, Shell interjected in a soothing tone. "Lee, it's okay. I've had a really long day, I'm tired and I just wanna sleep now. I've done all the talking I can for one day. We can have a chat tomorrow before I leave, alright? I promise."

Removing her hand from Lee's arm, Shell added, "Now what's your number?"

Lee looked at the back of his flip phone to see a small handwritten phone number on a piece of paper attached to the phone. "Can never remember." He passed the phone to Shell, who promptly pressed his number into her own phone to call him. After it rang, she hung up and passed his flip phone back to him.

"There you go. Save my number to your contacts. I'll do the same." Shell instructed. Lee followed suit and then put his flip phone back on the bed.

Shell put her phone back in her trouser pocket. "I'm just across the hall if you need me, okay?"

Lee nodded, appreciative of Shell's concern.

Glancing down at the wreckage of plastic bags and uneaten food strewn across the thin carpet, Shell frowned. "Oh, sorry about the mess. Here, I'll sort it."

As Shell bent forward to start gathering the items, Lee hastily stopped her. "No no, it's fine, I'll clean it before I go to bed."

Shell looked uncertain. "You sure?"

Lee nodded resolutely. "Yeah, yeah, it's fine." He suddenly recalled something Shell had previously said to him. "Wait, hang on a sec. That guy you mentioned earlier..." His voice trailed off as he tried to remember the name.

"What guy?"

"The one with the surname no one knows, what was his name again?"

"Oh, Robbie?" Shell offered.

Lee snapped his fingers. "Yeah, yeah."

Shell tilted her head. "What about him?"

Lee leaned in closer, his eyes narrowing. "Was he the abusive boyfriend you were with?"

Shell nodded slowly. "Yeah, why? Do you remember him?"

"It could be the same guy, I'm not too sure," Lee said. "There was someone we heard about who was a proper nutter. Big fella. Hard as nails. Woman beater..."

Shell inhaled sharply. "Yeah, yeah!" she interjected.

"He tried getting with Paul's cousin," Lee continued. "Think his name was Robbie."

"When was this?" Shell asked, her breath quickening.

"Oh, was years ago now, like at least six years I think." Lee estimated.

Shell bit her lip. "What happened?"

"Paul told her to stay away from him. He found out Robbie was really high up, like, he had family connections in MI5 and that's why he kept his surname quiet..." Lee leaned in even closer now, his voice dropping to a haunting whisper. "And apparently he killed an escort too."

Shell's eyes flew open in horror. "Fuck off, it is him yeah, that's my ex, Robbie!" She buried her face in her hands. "He used to brag about killing a sex worker and getting away with it. I just thought it was all talk. Jesus."

Lee scratched his chin pensively. "Did Mark know you were with him?"

"No, thank fuck," Shell shook her head. "He hated every lad I went out with anyway."

Lee chuckled at the recollection. "Yeah, that sounds like Mark. Very protective."

A wistful smile played on Shell's lips as she too plunged into nostalgia. "Honest to God, you should've seen him every time I brought a different lad home from school."

Lee's curiosity was piqued. "Why, what did he do?"

"He wanted to see how strong they all were if they were gonna look after me, so they had to pass this stupid little test he made them do. They had to do like fifty push ups while he was showing off his physique, it was so funny!"

"Anything to scare them off!" Lee said, while chuckling to himself.

"Yeah, exactly!" Shell replied, following suit with barrels of laughter, the darkness of the entire evening momentarily broken.

Shell yawned, the lateness of the hour settling in. Lee still appeared animated, like he wanted to prolong their conversation.

"Good times..." Shell mumbled. "Anyway, I'm gonna go bed now. Don't even care what time it is. I'm knackered."

Lee glanced down at his wristwatch. "It's only quarter to nine."

Shell let out an exasperated sigh and made her way towards the door. Lee watched her, hoping she would change her mind.

"Sounds about right," Shell sighed. "Speak to you in the morning, Lee. Goodnight."

Lee hesitated, seeming not quite ready to part ways. "Er - yeah, goodnight, Shell."

Shell pulled the door open with a creak and stepped out into the dim hallway, letting it fall shut behind her with a definitive thud. Her footsteps receded as she entered her own hotel room.

Lee continued staring at the closed door, struggling to process the tumultuous events of the day. He then glanced down at the mess on the floor and decided to clean it up, which he duly did.

9

Shell entered Room 48.

Dropping her heavy handbag, Shell pulled out several items: her bible, loved from frequent reading; her journal containing her entire investigation surrounding Lee's whereabouts; and the bottle of water she had taken from his gym bag, representing a hope that her deepest thirst may still need to be quenched.

With a sense of ritual, Shell kissed the bible and lined it up neatly with the other sparse belongings she called her own in this temporary home. Her few treasures arranged carefully on the cheap bedspread, she then retrieved Lee's steak knife and a voice recorder from her bag.

Shell's pulse quickened as she switched off the flashing red light on the device and pressed play with trembling fingers. Crackling through the speaker came her voice, followed by Lee's.

"Lee? Lee Barker?"

"Yeah?"

"My name is Shell. We've never met before, but...can I come in, please? We need to talk."

Relief washed over Shell as she let out a breath she didn't realise she was holding.

Later, with the moon high in the night sky, Shell twisted in her scratchy hotel sheets, chasing sleep as an adversary lurking ever out of reach.

Across the hall from Shell, Lee laid stiffly on top of his own bed linens. Fully dressed in his rumpled clothing as if sleep were an unwanted guest, he fixated on the cracks in the water-stained ceiling. His mind churned too, anxiety and trepidation his sole companions in the gloom.

The morning sunlight - attempting to crack through the autumn clouds - accompanied the sound of birds singing, filling the air outside The Puppet Master Hotel.

In the car park, the Ford Mondeo had parked up a few spaces away from Lee's rented Fiesta and Michael Kingham's Volvo. It stayed there the entire night.

The drawn curtain in Shell's room kept shadows at bay but did little to illuminate her path ahead. She stirred, awakened by the jarring ringtone of her phone skidding across the weathered dresser next to the bed.

Clearing the sleepy gravel from her throat, Shell threw herself out of bed and grabbed the phone, accepting the call from the man who was only just a few yards away from her in Room 47.

"Morning, Lee, you alright? How did you sleep?"

"Hi, yeah, er - could you come over as soon as you're ready, please?" Even over the line, the tension in Lee's voice was palpable.

Canvassing her nerves, Shell confirmed she would meet Lee shortly. Anticipation launched her into a familiar routine.

Three resounding knocks echoed from the door, rousing Lee from his restless doze. He fumbled as he rose from the rumpled sheets, pausing to smooth the wrinkles of yesterday's clothes.

Lee pulled open the door to find Shell loitering in the hallway, handbag clutched to her side with her right hand embedded inside it.

Lee noticed that Shell was also wearing the same clothes as the previous day.

"Morning!" Shell said, in an upbeat manner.

"Morning." Lee responded, rather unenthusiastically.

Shell's gaze bored into Lee as he wordlessly stepped aside. She strode sharply across the faded carpet, then positioned herself in the centre of the room facing him.

Lee shoved the door closed and approached Shell.

"Everything alright?" Shell questioned.

Lee's eyes skittered away from Shell's stare, a flush rising to colour his sallow cheeks. "I couldn't sleep." he stated, clearly discomforted by her presence.

Shell dipped her chin in understanding, a wry smile twisting her lips. "Last night was a lot."

The flush on Lee's face deepened at the reminder, his shoulders hunching inward defensively. "Yeah, it was." he conceded faintly, the words barely audible in the quiet room.

Impatience sharpened Shell's tone when she pressed, "So what's up?" She took a half-step nearer, intruding into Lee's personal space.

"You woke me at half five in the morning, Lee. What's going on?"

Lee wrestled visibly for words, his throat working though nothing emerged. Beads of sweat prickled at his receding hairline as Shell's expectant stare weighed the air between them.

After an interminable wait, Lee managed to rasp, "I need to tell you something." His hands twisted nervously in the fabric of his wrinkled shirt.

Shell's glare intensified, honing in on Lee like a lioness sighting helpless prey. "Okay." she nearly growled, a wealth of menace buried in that single word.

But Lee's attention had shifted, his eyes narrowing at where Shell's hand yet lingered inside the dark recesses of her handbag. "What's in the bag?" he questioned sharply, body tensing. "Why is your hand in there? What are you holding?"

Tension sang in the air as Shell slowly withdrew her journal from the bag's depths. "Oh, it's my journal," she hastened to explain off Lee's look. "I just like the feel of it," Her lips quivered with feigned humour. "Wanna touch? It's dead smooth."

Lee scowled down at the proffered book. "No, thanks. I'm fine." he bit out tersely, clearly unmoved by Shell's pandering tone.

Shell's smile faded, the light mood evaporating. "Suit yourself." she allowed coolly, returning the journal to her bag though her hand still remained inside. Her body had shifted subtly, exuding the mien of a watcher waiting for their chance to strike.

"Come on then," Shell directed sharply when Lee volunteered no further information. "What's up? I'm not gonna ask again, Lee."

As Lee visibly gathered the scraps of his courage, Shell's hand shifted ever so slightly within the dark confines of her handbag.

Lee's shoulders slumped in resignation. "That quote from the bible. It was all I could think about after you left last night. You said you feel responsible for giving Mark the closure he needs. I do too. Mark deserves to rest in peace."

Lee finally met Shell's eyes. She could see the guilt swirling within.

"I'm sorry that you spent so long trying to find me, but...It all ends now."

Shell noticed Lee's admission carried a ring of finality. Her hand slid deeper into the bag's depths. Whatever Lee was about to say to her, she finally felt like she hadn't wasted her time with everything. It all came down to this.

"To whom much is given, much is required..." Lee took a steadying breath before continuing. "Shell, I'm sorry I lied to you last night. My guard was up. But this is the truth."

Shell sensed Lee was telling the truth but braced for impact. Years of hardship had taught her a partial truth could still conceal a deeper betrayal.

Lee inhaled deeply as Shell stared blankly into the distance, her mind clearly a thousand miles away.

"After I dropped Mark off in Tottenham," Lee continued tentatively, "I got pulled over by the police...The officer that stopped me was Peter Dean."

A puzzled expression flickered across Shell's face. "Who's Peter Dean?"

Lee's gaze dropped to the floor, his face awash with shame and regret. "The guy that quit when we lived in the YMCA."

Slow realization dawned on Shell's face, morphing from confusion to clarity and finally to anger.

"No, Lee. Don't," Shell said, slowly shaking her head in disbelief. She took a deep breath, composing herself to allow Lee to go on.

"They were onto us. We were being followed and they were closing in," Lee confessed. "It was only a matter of time."

Shell gritted her teeth. "And you didn't tell Mark?"

"No." Lee admitted, finally meeting Shell's gaze though unable to hold it for long under her fiery glare.

"Why?" Shell demanded through clenched teeth.

"Peter knew our history. He knew the others didn't stand a chance. I never had a criminal record and he knew I wasn't involved in the drug side of things," Lee rationalized quickly. "He told me to stay quiet and I had to leave before the next deal happened."

Shell nodded slowly. "So he gave you a friendly warning?"

"Yeah."

"What was in it for you?"

"Immunity from prosecution." Lee confessed softly, dropping his gaze in shame once more.

Shell chuckled mirthlessly, a wide grin spreading across her face as the pieces fell into place. She stopped herself from giving in to the urge to laugh out loud, instead looking briefly up at the ceiling to gather her composure before staring Lee up and down. Her hand remained buried in her bag the whole time.

"I knew it, I fucking knew it." Shell muttered under her breath.

"Shell, I -" Lee began pleadingly before being cut off.

"No. Don't. Don't you dare." Shell interjected sharply, pointing an accusatory finger with her left hand.

"I'm sorry." Lee offered weakly.

Shell clenched her fist, pressing her lips together tightly. "You're sorry? Okay. Okay, you're sorry. Now what?"

Lee hesitated, scrambling for the right words. "I didn't have a choice, Shell. Even if I did tell

Mark or any of the others, they would've accused me of going behind their back anyway. No one in the drug world admits they've spoken to the police. Doesn't work like that. Plus, it could've been a test."

Shell laughed derisively. "You know what? That was quite a performance you put on last night with that whole sob story about your life being so hard, saying I had no right to question you after finding out your best friend died, telling me that your memory had gone to shit. I actually felt sorry for you…I knew you were lying, Lee. I guess I just wanted to believe you."

Lee shifted uncomfortably, clearly regretting his moment of truth.

"I said it all along. I tried telling Mark you had something to do with it, but he wouldn't listen. Yeah, you technically didn't have anything to do with the raid itself, but knowing about it for as long as you did and only thinking about yourself? They all walked into the lion's den and you did nothing…That makes you more slimy than Peter Dean and every other bent copper out there." Shell chuckled bitterly.

"I mean, 'immunity from prosecution'? Who the fuck do you think you are? That's why you're *really* on the run, isn't it? You're running from the family you betrayed. The five men who accepted you as one of their own. The five men you took a million quid from and then ran for the hills when time was up!"

Lee stood motionless, like a child being scolded by an angry parent. Shell took a step towards him, the tension in the air unbearable.

"Rest assured, Lee...Mark is now turning in his grave."

"I gave you what you wanted, Shell. I told you the truth." Lee protested weakly.

"Yes, you did. Congratulations."

"And you promised me you're not gonna turn me in."

"That's right, I did promise you that," Shell nodded slowly. "But it seems like your best mate Peter has already taken care of that, hasn't he?"

Shell turned away from Lee, walking towards the window, eyeing her handbag briefly before facing him again.

"I mean, even if I did go to the police now, what good would it do? It would be my word against yours. My word against Peter's. I wouldn't stand a chance, come on."

Shell was now feeling as if she was a cat; seeing Lee as the cornered mouse.

"Let's face it, Lee. I don't have any evidence to prove the police granted you freedom in exchange for my brother getting sent down, do I? You only told me the truth because you felt safe to do so...But you should know by now, Lee, I do all of my research. Did you really think I was just going to interrogate you and then disappear as if nothing happened?"

Fear flickered across Lee's face. "What do you mean?"

Shell reached into her trouser pocket with her left hand, pulling out her small recording device. She pressed a button to stop the flashing red recording light. Then she pressed play.

"Morning!" came Shell's recorded voice.

"Morning." Lee's voice replied flatly through the tiny speaker.

Lee froze, eyes wide with shock. Shell clicked stop and slipped the device back into her pocket.

"My dad heard everything. All the audio from last night and right now has been sent to his cloud account...It's game over, Lee."

Tears filled Lee's eyes but his expression remained unreadable. Pure rage blended with resignation, perhaps? He appeared on the verge of a panic attack.

Shell began edging slowly towards the door, wary of Lee. Her right hand stayed hidden in her bag.

"My dad's probably called the police by now. There's nothing you can do. I'm leaving, okay?" Shell kept her eyes locked on Lee as she sidled closer to the door and potential escape.

"No, you - I don't..." Lee stammered helplessly, struggling to breathe.

Before Shell could bolt for the door, Lee suddenly lunged at her with alarming speed, slamming her against the wall, easily overpowering her.

Lee grabbed Shell's shirt with one mighty hand while raising a clenched fist with the other, hesitating. His face was terrifying but Shell stayed calm, her right hand clutching the handle of Lee's steak knife inside her bag, ready to strike back if needed.

They were at an impasse, Lee battling himself, aware he had physically threatened his best friend's sister. Shell peered desperately into Lee's wild eyes, knowing she was prepared to fight for her life.

"Don't do it, Lee. Let me go." Shell warned, voice shaking slightly. She grabbed his clenched fist with her left hand. "Get off."

Lee relaxed his grip and stepped back. Shell gently pushed against his chest to widen the space between them and removed her right hand from her handbag. She had kept the steak knife inside the bag, confident that Lee no longer posed a threat to her.

"What have I done?" Lee sobbed, distraught.

Shell held him at arm's length, regaining her composure. "Stay there and don't move a fucking muscle, I swear to God."

Lee struggled to control himself as he looked up towards the ceiling. "I'm so sorry, Mark. I didn't mean it, I didn't mean it. Shell, I'm sorry, I'm so sorry, I'm sorry, I'm -"

His legs buckled abruptly and he stumbled backwards, half-sitting, half-collapsing onto the bed behind him. He closed his eyes, overcome.

"I don't wanna do this anymore, Mark, I wanna go home, I wanna go home, please, Mark, please-" Lee babbled indistinctly.

"Lee. Lee, listen to me," Shell called firmly.

Lee's muttering died down as he swayed gently with his eyes still closed. Shell kept her distance.

"Lee!"

Lee's eyes blinked open. "Yeah, yeah," he mumbled dully.

"Can you hear me?"

"Yeah." Lee nodded.

"Calm the fuck down."

"Okay, okay."

"Take a deep breath."

"Okay." Lee closed his eyes again and inhaled deeply before slowly exhaling.

"Right, now look at me." Shell instructed.

Lee met Shell's gaze steadily this time.

"Nearly gave yourself a heart attack." Shell admonished.

"I'm fine, I'm fine." Lee insisted weakly.

"Listen to me. I'm gonna go now, okay?"

"Okay."

"It's done. You know that, right?"

Lee nodded. "Yeah, I know." His voice was a dull monotone. He couldn't bring himself to meet Shell's eyes to see the judgement there, or worse yet, the pity.

Shell stepped towards Lee, her slight frame tense. "Don't try running away again," she said, an edge sharpening her words. "Just give yourself up when the police get here, okay?"

Lee's throat appeared to restrict as he whispered "I will, I will."

Shell studied Lee's downturned face for a long moment before turning towards the door. She paused with her hand on the tarnished brass doorknob. "If you have any chance of redeeming yourself, just wait here," she said quietly. "Don't cause a scene. Don't lie," A heavy silence filled the dingy little room. "Do it for Mark."

At the mention of Mark's name, Lee flinched as if he'd been struck. He pressed his lips together, unable to respond around the hard knot in his throat. Shell searched his face once more, before slipping out the door without another word.

The sharp click of the latch striking home jolted Lee from his stupor. As the door swung slowly shut behind Shell, he rose unsteadily to his feet, swaying for a moment before turning towards the bed where his gym bags lay in a careless heap. His movements were mechanical as he unzipped the bags and began rifling through their contents with increasing desperation. It was time to end his suffering.

A moment of hesitation.

The steak knife was missing.

Lee frantically looked around the room, under the bed and on the floor before making his way to the bathroom.

Standing before the bathroom sink, Lee's reflection gazed back at him with an intensity that mirrored his inner turmoil. A wave of realisation washed over him, etching lines of understanding onto his features. With a subtle nod, a smirk danced across his lips.

"Shell." Lee whispered, realising that she had taken his knife.

But the calm facade shattered like fragile glass as Lee's body rebelled against him. He staggered toward the toilet, the familiar churning in his stomach signalling the inevitable. Dropping to his knees, he leaned over the bowl, his body convulsing as he expelled the contents of his stomach.

10

Shell hurried down the hallway, her shoes scuffing softly against the carpet.

Gripping her phone tightly, Shell tapped out a number with her thumb. Her heart pounded with adrenaline even as her narrow shoulders sagged under the weight of exhaustion and stress.

The hallway stood empty and silent, the only light coming from the fixture mounted halfway down the hall, its buttery glow not quite reaching the dark corners near the ceiling. Up ahead, the brass handles of a heavy wooden door glinted. Pushing through it, Shell emerged at the top of the staircase leading down to the hotel lobby.

Shell adjusted the strap of her shoulder bag as it draped across her body, feeling the small, hard edge of the voice recorder through the brown faux leather.

In the reception area, Shell paced, irritation radiating from the furrow of her brow as she held her phone to her ear.

The unoccupied desk of the receptionist lay silent as Shell passed, her movements purposeful. Placing her room key card on the desk, she continued toward the exit.

Outside, in the hotel car park, Shell attempted another call, frustration evident in her voice as she left a voicemail.

"Dad, I know it's nearly six in the morning, but answer your phone. I've got so much to tell you, you're not gonna believe it," Shell pleaded into the device. "I'm leaving the hotel now, should be back home just before seven. I've got two recordings you need to listen to, but basically, he told me everything."

Shell continued. "He knew about the raid because one of Mark's old mates from years ago is now a copper and he told Lee about it, but there's loads more you'll hear when I get home. Call me as soon as you get this, alright? Love you, bye."

As Shell ended her voice message, she put her phone back inside her handbag as she walked past the mysterious Ford Mondeo that, unbeknownst to her, had been parked a couple of spaces away from her dad's Volvo all night.

A figure swiftly emerged from the Mondeo, towering and menacing, his slick black hair bouncing with each purposeful step he took. Shell's heart pounded in her chest as she turned to see Robbie charging toward her with demonic rage manifesting his entire being.

"Come here, you fucking bitch!" Robbie's voice sliced through the air, venom dripping from every syllable.

Terror coursed through Shell as Robbie lunged, his grip tight around her waist with his other hand slapped over her mouth to prevent her from screaming.

"You fucking little cunt! You're not getting away this time. I told you this would happen if–"

Shell fought back, sinking her teeth into Robbie's fingers, eliciting a scream of pain. But his hold remained firm, his fingers snaking around her hair, wrenching her head back.

Desperation fueled Shell's struggle as she tried to free herself, her screams echoing in the empty air, trying desperately to open her handbag that was still strapped over her right shoulder down to her left hip.

Robbie pulled Shell closer to him and with his other hand, now a clenched fist, he landed a heavy punch to her left eye.

Robbie's continuous blows rained down relentlessly, each of them connecting as a cruel punctuation mark on her torment.

Shell fell down onto the hard concrete. Robbie began using his lower extremities to inflict more pain onto her, such as kicking her repeatedly and even stomping down his thick black boots onto her stomach and flailing arms.

In a final act of brutality, Robbie rendered Shell unconscious with a vicious kick to the face. He lifted her limp body up and cradled her in his arms as he carried her to the waiting Mondeo. With chilling efficiency, he deposited her in the boot before slamming it shut.

Robbie returned to the driver's seat, started the engine and then sped away.

The Ford Mondeo disappeared into the pre-dawn gloom, The Puppet Master Hotel a silent witness to the horrors that had unfolded in its shadow.

As Lee gripped the toilet bowl with trembling hands, he emptied the meagre contents of his stomach in painful heaves. When the last wave of nausea passed, he inhaled a quivering breath and spat residual bile into the bowl before flushing it away.

Lifting his head, he caught his reflection in the bathroom mirror and cringed. His skin held a sickly, sallow tinge. Dark circles haunted his bloodshot eyes.

Running a hand over his clammy face, he shuddered out another breath. His fingers followed the hard line of his jaw, calloused pads scraping over day-old stubble.

The tiny bathroom echoed with emptiness, the cracked tile floor offering no comfort. Lee felt the familiar silence return once more.

Turning from the mirror, he avoided the reflection of his weakness and fumbled for the door handle after grabbing the bath towel on the floor, desperate to escape the confined space.

Lee exited the bathroom, wiping his mouth with the towel before gently throwing it onto the crumpled sheets of his bed.

He strode over to the window. Peering outside, brows lifting in surprise having noticed the Volvo was still parked in the same spot.

"Oh, she's still here." Lee said, under his breath.

Puzzled, he turned from the window and stood motionless in the centre of the room, staring at the door.

"She left, didn't she?" he muttered, lost in thought.

Lee knocked sharply on the door of Room 48, the sound echoing faintly down the vacant hallway. Craning his neck, he pressed an ear to the wooden door.

"Shell?" he called. "You there?"

Lee pounded the door with three loud knocks that seemed to reverberate through the empty corridor. "Shell!"

After a brief moment with no response, he fished his flip phone from the pocket of his wrinkled trousers. He dialled a number and held the phone to one ear, his other ear still flush against the silent door. Hearing nothing within the room and the phone still ringing unanswered, he ended the call and pivoted back towards his own room, having left his door ajar.

Shutting his hotel room door decisively, Lee returned to the window and scanned the view outside with a brooding expression. He started to dial his phone again but halted abruptly, hand poised in midair.

"Wait a minute. What am I doing?" he said, staring down at the phone screen. "Why am I wasting my time? The police could be here soon."

He placed the phone onto the bed next to the crumpled towel. His gaze travelled over the room and settled on the pair of gym bags at the foot of the bed. He sighed heavily.

"So she took the knife, okay..."

Pacing the confines of the small room, Lee shook his head.

"There's no fucking way I'm going to prison, not a chance," he declared vehemently. "Over my dead body."

Halting by the bed, his darting eyes fixed upon the towel. In a decisive moment, he snatched it up, swiftly twisting and winding the fabric until it resembled a makeshift rope.

"This will have to do."

Clutching the towel rope in both hands, Lee surveyed the room, features taut with grim intent as he sought a place to secure it. His gaze travelled from bed frame to window to the metal curtain rod suspended over the large pane of glass.

Yes, that would suffice.

Glaring at the rickety chair against the wall, Lee devised a plan. With the chair scraping loudly across the floor, Lee situated it perfectly underneath the rod. He tested the rod's strength by climbing onto the chair and hanging his weight upon it. The metal held fast. The chair? Not so much.

After climbing down, he grabbed the towel rope. With practised efficiency he fashioned it into a noose, wrapping the coarse fabric in coils around his thin neck.

Lee drew a deep breath and cast one last sweeping survey over the dingy room that had been his home these past couple of days.

"Now or never," he whispered. "You can do this."

With stoic purpose, Lee mounted the chair, looped the loose end of the noose over the metal rod and yanked it down.

Still wearing yesterday's black socks, Lee carefully wedged his right foot against the window to maintain balance atop the unstable chair. He looped the towel tighter in an intricate hangman's knot.

Facing the barren room, Lee stared critically down at the floor, balancing his weight on the chair. He raised one foot tentatively, poising it over the carpet. Abruptly he drew back, features creasing with uncertainty and the first inkling of panic. Slow breaths rasped loud in the silence.

Attempting to pull himself together, Lee grabbed at the rod with both hands and hoisted himself higher so that his body dangled freely. The sudden movement dislodged the precarious chair, toppling it sideways to the floor with a clatter that shattered the room's oppressive hush.

Instant regret flooded Lee's chalk-white face. Suspended fully by his hands now clenched on the rod, stark terror gripped him.

Turning his body awkwardly, his feet scrabbling in search of impossible purchase, Lee twisted around to face the window. Grunting with effort, he tried bracing his feet on the glass to give his quivering arms some respite.

Suddenly both feet lost traction.

Lee slammed against the window with bruising force, biting back a cry as his body dropped dangerously closer towards the inevitable.

Only the desperate, waning strength of his fingers hooked on the rod saved Lee from the long plunge downward. Tears of pain leaked from the corners of his eyes as his fingers slowly, inexorably began sliding from their tenuous grip. Time was running out.

With an air of doom, Lee watched his whitened fingers slip free of the rod. His body recoiled, twisting sideways once more to face the empty room as gravity claimed him.

Feet cycling futilely mere inches from the floor, Lee clawed frantically at the noose, seeking to wedge even one small gap of merciful air.

Above him, the knot fastening the noose to the rod started to give way under his jerking death throes. As darkness crept into his vision, Lee sensed himself lowering gradually closer to the floor. With a final burst of defiant energy, he stretched his toes downwards, straining for even the barest brush of carpet beneath his socks.

Just as unconsciousness rushed up to swallow Lee into its beckoning void, a visual silhouette of a man appeared in front of him.

It looked like Mark. It couldn't be though, surely? Whoever, or whatever, it was - it certainly made its presence known in that split second. Lee could swear he heard a bellowing cry of "NO!" from the silhouette before it vanished as quickly as it arrived.

Almost instantly, the knot around the curtain rod unravelled completely.

Lee collapsed to the floor in a limp tangle of limbs. Inhaling in great rasping gulps, he tore the noose violently from his mottled throat and crawled on hands and knees to the sanctuary of his bed.

Sprawled atop the sheets, chest heaving, Lee stared blankly upward as blessed air flowed back into his starving lungs. Gradually his frantic gasps eased into steadier breaths.

Was that Mark? Did Mark somehow intervene from the afterlife, or was it something as rational as the brain going into overdrive due to a lack of oxygen? Whatever the correct answer was, Mark's death was now weighing heavy on Lee's mind. The disturbing irony of almost succumbing to a similar fate as his best friend, struggling to breathe in his final moments, washed over Lee like a painful reminder of his own mortality.

The sound of his flip phone receiving a call snapped Lee out of his state of senselessness.

Scrubbing the tears from his cheeks, he sat up and reached for his buzzing phone.

"Hello?" He croaked, wincing at the grating pain in his abused throat.

On the other end of the line, Shell's panicked voice broke through bursts of static.

"Shell? What's - I can't hear you, you keep breaking up, where are you?" Lee demanded urgently. "Can you hear me?"

More distorted words rang through the receiver, faint but carrying a note of hysteria.

Lee stiffened, features igniting with alarm. "Calm down, I can't understand, did you just say Robbie?"

As Shell's fragmented reply came through, Lee shot to his feet, phone still glued to his ear. "Oh my God."

Lee began dragging on his shoes as Shell continued her broken narrative. "Okay, okay, I'm leaving now, stay on the phone with me."

Phone pinned between ear and shoulder, Lee asked briskly, "Yes, I'm just getting my shoes on now, stay with me, okay? Are you badly hurt?"

Hefting both gym bags, Lee sprinted for the door as Shell responded in choked whimpers. Wrenching the door open, Lee fled from the room that had so very nearly become his tomb.

Lee raced in a panic down the hallway, his footsteps thudding on the thin carpet. Cradling his phone to his ear with one sweaty hand, he struggled to keep hold of the two overstuffed gym bags swinging heavily in his other arm.

"I'm going as fast as I can!" Lee panted into the phone, nearly stumbling over his own feet. "Don't hang up!"

Bursting through the stairwell door, Lee vaulted down the steps, taking them two at a time. The bags banged painfully against his ribs with each landing. Still somehow keeping his phone pressed to his ear, he ran through the empty reception and burst out of the hotel's entrance into the car park.

Lee spotted his rental car sitting faithfully next to the Volvo. It was only at this moment where he felt a strong sense of anger. Anger towards himself for not protecting Mark's little sister when she needed it the most. From this point on, Lee was going to do anything in order to protect Shell at all costs.

Juggling keys, bags, and phone, Lee managed to pop open the boot and fling the bags inside before slamming it shut.

He raced around to the driver's side door and folded himself inside. Jamming the keys in the ignition, the engine sputtered to life.

Wheels spinning for purchase on the tarmac, with a sharp turn he sped out of the car park, nearly clipping the front of the Volvo.

With his phone still glued to his ear, he raced away like an eager Formula One Champion.

If anyone had been watching from one of the many windows of the vast Puppet Master Hotel, they'd have been treated to the screeching departure of two vehicles early that morning.

11

The serene tranquillity of the River Weaver Bridge, with its endless expanse of lush greenery and murky waters, was abruptly shattered by the arrival of a speeding Ford Mondeo.

The car screeched to a halt a few yards from the riverbank, its presence an ominous disruption to the natural beauty of the surroundings.

Robbie emerged from the car, still consumed by palpable rage. His anger radiated like a fiery aura, casting a shadow over the peaceful scene.

"Wakey-wakey!" Robbie's voice cut through the air like a whip, laced with venomous contempt. "Don't want you to miss what I've got planned for you. Wake up!"

Robbie's words dripped with malice as he approached the back of the car, his movements brimming with violent intent.

With a forceful gesture, Robbie slammed his fist down onto the boot of the car, before he yanked open the rear passenger door.

"Do you have any fucking idea how much shit you got yourself in when you left me, hey?" Robbie's voice was a menacing growl as he retrieved lengths of thick rope and duct tape from the car's interior, laying them out onto the roof with cruel precision. "I fucking told you exactly what would happen if you ever walked out on me, didn't I?"

Robbie's threats hung in the air like a dark omen, a chilling reminder of the consequences of defiance. "You remember? That other slag tried doing the same thing to me and look what happened to her!"

With a sadistic grin, Robbie reminisced over his past atrocities, relishing in the fear that had flickered in his victim's eyes.

"She vanished off the face of the earth and now it's your turn!" Robbie bellowed out.

From within the confines of the car's boot, Shell's muffled cries pierced the air, a desperate plea for salvation. She also tried everything she could to escape by kicking and punching the walls of her makeshift prison, to no avail.

"HELP! HELP ME! OH GOD! PLEASE!" Shell's voice trembled with terror.

Robbie's twisted amusement only grew as he revelled in Shell's anguish, his deathly smile betraying the depths of his depravity.

"LET ME OUT! PLEASE!"

"Sorry, Shell, what was that?" Robbie's voice dripped with mockery as he leaned in closer, savouring Shell's torment. "I can't hear you properly, what did you say?"

"ROBBIE! I CAN'T BREATHE!"

Robbie rested his elbow onto the boot. "Isn't that funny? I'm sure those were your brother's last words as well, weren't they?"

Shell continued to scream and kick even louder now, finally accepting that her chances of survival were slim to none.

"Hey, hey, come on, shush! You need to save your oxygen. You haven't got much in there, have you?" Robbie taunted.

"I FUCKING HATE YOU! LET ME OUT!"

Robbie started laughing as he walked back to the rear passenger's open door.

The car was now violently shaking from Shell's indomitable struggle. This prompted Robbie to continue throwing further insults towards her. "God, where was all this fight when I'd fuck you, hey? Would've loved holding you down watching you fight back like this!"

As Robbie retrieved his final item from the car - a jerry can - he resigned himself of all emotion, a rarity for him.

"Hey Shell! Remember that time you told me we lost our spark?"

"FUCK YOU ROBBIE!" Shell screamed, refusing to give up the fight of her life.

Robbie smirked briefly, slightly admiring Shell's determination. "Well, today's your lucky day, because I found that spark again."

The sudden pause in the kicking and shouting from within the boot was confirmation to him.

She gets it. She fucking gets it.

Robbie began whistling a monotonic tune as he was tipping petrol from the jerry can all over the Mondeo. He walked around the entire perimeter of the car, making sure every part was completely doused in petrol until the container was empty.

Shell resumed her kicking and banging but Robbie noticed there was much less vigour behind her fight. Her oxygen would now be dangerously low. He heard a barely audible threat from Shell.

Robbie tossed aside the empty jerry can and stood back to admire his work. He proudly walked to the boot of the car again, having heard Shell's muffled voice. "What was that?"

"I said...I'm gonna fucking kill you." Shell repeated.

Finding Shell's pitiful threat amusing, Robbie couldn't help but let out a brief chuckle. "Is that right? You're gonna kill me, yeah?"

"I swear to God, I will." Shell's tone was filled with a darkness that Robbie had never heard from her before.

Observing the overall situation, he decided to take things to another level of extreme torture.

To Robbie, it simply wasn't enough to set the car alight with Shell trapped inside the boot, oh no, that would be too easy.

In order to completely satisfy his deranged ego, Robbie had to kick it up a notch. He had already killed a woman in this manner before, so now it only felt right for him to inflict more unnecessary damage.

He came prepared for such an exhilarating experience. He pulled out a pair of swimming goggles and a cigarette lighter from his jacket pocket.

Robbie called out to Shell once more. "Shell, how do you expect to kill me when all you have on you in that handbag is pepper spray and a journal?"

Shell remained quiet. Robbie's eyebrows raised, anticipating some kind of response.

"Yeah, I thought so. I know more than you think, Shell," Robbie proclaimed. "My family has been keeping me up to date on where you've been, what you carry with you and even where you sleep at night...I always win."

Robbie continued speaking, this time in a more cheerful tone, adding his final touch of mockery by doing so. "Come on Shell, you're about to be reunited with your twat of a brother. This should be a joyous occasion, cheer up!"

Robbie walked closer to the car, putting his cigarette lighter back into his jacket pocket. "As a parting gift, feel free to go nuts with that pepper spray, if you want?"

Adjusting the swimming goggles until they were ready to be worn comfortably, Robbie's arrogance remained ever so present.

"Just do me a favour though, will you?" Robbie gestured, while stretching the swimming goggles out with both hands before bringing it down over his head like a royal crown. "When you get to hell, give Mark my regards."

Robbie securely placed the plastic goggles over his eyes, convinced that Shell's pepper spray would now be rendered useless.

Stepping forward to the car, Robbie grabbed the lip of the boot and pushed the button underneath to unlock it.

Preparing for Shell to squirt the pepper spray into his face, Robbie quickly lifted the boot lid fully open, even moving his face forward in a mocking gesture, as if to say, 'here you go, bitch, surprise'.

He was even mindful to keep his mouth tightly closed to avoid taking in a gob full of the spray which could easily incapacitate the recipient.

Shell sensed Robbie's presence at the rear of the car.

Half a pound of Twopenny rice...

She heard his hand making contact with the boot lid.

Half a pound of treacle... That's the way the money goes...

The boot lid popped and was swiftly raised. The immediate rush of daylight and fresh air had a similar effect on Shell as a cup of cold water in the face of an unexpecting sleeper.

"POP GOES THE WEASEL!" she roared, her right arm thrust upwards. The steak knife went straight into Robbie's jugular or carotid artery, Shell wasn't sure which, but it found its target like a darts player finding the bullseye to win the World Championship.

As Shell lay in the darkness of the boot of the car, desperately low on oxygen, and hearing her psycho ex splashing liquid around the car which she knew was petrol due to the smell seeping into her four-wheeled prison, she suddenly remembered a toy Jack-in-the-box which was bought for her one Christmas when she was a little girl, maybe six or seven, she couldn't recall.

But one thing she did recall was the tune the metal box used to play when the handle was turned. She has never forgotten that tune as she nearly shit herself the first time she tried it.

Half a Twopenny rice,
Half a pound of treacle,
That's the way the money goes...

On the next word - *POP* - the lid on the Jack-in-the-box used to spring up and the Jack clown thing within used to shoot up and make a wailing noise which sort of befit its ugly little face. She remembered scaring her young friends with it too. Such fun days.

In her oxygen deprived state, that horrible little Jack-in-the-box had almost come to her rescue. Shell became that little bastard.

But unlike the child's toy, when her lid popped, Shell was prepared to strike a lethal blow, not just scare her victim.

Despite grabbing Shell's wrist, Robbie's mouth remained widened with shock as the moment hung in the air, suspended in time as her victory became apparent.

With nothing but a gurgled gasp, Robbie stumbled backward after Shell mercilessly yanked the blade out of his neck, blood spurting and cascading down onto the grass beneath him.

Shell watched as Robbie fell down on the softened grass below, face up, knowing he was looking up to a place he was not heading to.

Shell's left eye was badly bruised and her cheeks and jaw were also slightly cut from Robbie's beating, particularly from the lethal kick to her face. Her handbag was still positioned across her body as it was when she was kidnapped.

Shell caught her breath as she fumbled out of the boot. Her knees buckled as she grabbed hold of the car to regain her balance.

She gazed down at her handiwork. The arterial spurt lessening as the fiend quickly bled out. The long lines and fine splashes of blood all around resembled a horror scene painted by Pablo Picasso.

She sidled up to the blood-soaked Robbie and squatted next to him to remove the goggles, designed to protect his eyes, completely useless for protecting a carotid artery from a jagged blade.

Shell taunted him some more by wiggling the knife over him. Drops of blood landed on his face and clothing, blending with the deluge already there.

"Didn't know about *this*, did you?"

Robbie tried to respond, but the pools of blood gushing out of his mouth made it impossible for him to do so.

"What's that? I can't hear you." Shell mimicked Robbie's earlier sarcastic tone.

Shell kept her eyes locked onto Robbie's as his movements ceased. Her face remained stoic as she refused to show him any other emotion. She wanted the last thing he ever saw to be the triumph in her eyes.

Robbie's life ended there and then.

Shell's breath came in ragged gasps, her hands trembling with adrenaline as she surveyed the scene before her.

As the reality of her actions sank in, she crumpled to the ground like a small child, tears streaming down her face in silent catharsis.

Amidst the chaos and turmoil, one thing remained clear. Shell had emerged victorious, her spirit unbroken by the darkness that sought to consume her.

Following a brief moment of reflection, she sprung into action.

So much to do.

Shell opened her handbag and fished out her phone before dropping the blood-stained knife back inside.

She stepped away from the inert body to make a call. She ignored the missed call notification that was on her screen and dialled another number. She waited. No answer.

This was no time to leave a voice message. Shell's frustration exploded in a blind flash. "DAD, ANSWER YOUR FUCKING PHONE!"

Shell continued crying as she disconnected the call, frustrated by not getting through to her dad for the second time that morning.

Without even thinking, Shell called the only other person that could potentially help her. The same person who had tried calling her when she was unconscious in Robbie's car boot.

She put the phone up to her ear once more, trying to calm herself down, taking deep breaths and hoping this call would be answered.

It worked. Lee answered the call.

"Lee! Thank God, you have to come get me, please, please I need your help. I'm in a field next to a river and a bridge, I think it's the River Weaver. Lee, can you hear me? Robbie kidnapped me!"

Shell's words desperately bellowed down the phone. Unfortunately, the poor signal kept cutting her off.

"Lee? Yes, Robbie kidnapped me in the car park. I've just killed Robbie, he's dead, I stabbed him, I stabbed him! Please hurry, Lee!" Even Shell couldn't believe her own words.

"I'm fine, I'm fine, but Robbie's dead, so I'm okay. Thank you, Lee. I'm not hanging up, I'm not." Shell said, finally composing herself.

12

The sun tried ever so desperately to peek through the countless clouds in the sky that towered over the vast fields next to the River Weaver. Shell stood with her phone pressed to her ear, having moved even further from Robbie's body, which lay flat on the grass next to the riverbank. As she waved at the approaching Fiesta across the field, her panic seemed to retreat behind a mask of forced calm.

"Yeah, I see you now." Shell said into the phone before ending the call and dropping it into her handbag.

The car skidded to a halt nearby and Lee scrambled out, his face etched with concern. After slamming the door shut, he headed directly for Shell, eyes darting towards the darkness that awaited them by the river. "Are you okay?" he asked.

Shell nodded, the shadow of her bruises darkening her left eye and cheeks. "Yeah."

Lee frowned. "Are you sure? That's one hell of a black eye."

"I'm fine, honestly, don't worry about it."

They walked slowly through the ankle high grass, the atmosphere tense. Lee's eyes kept flicking to Shell's bruised face.

After a moment, Shell said quietly, "Thanks for coming, Lee."

"It's okay. I'm just glad you called me when you did. I don't know what would've happened if..." Lee's words trailed off as his gaze moved to the river.

Shell stopped abruptly, and Lee stood still beside her. She took a breath before speaking, her tone carefully controlled.

"Alright, look. We didn't exactly end things well back at the hotel. So before I get you involved in all this, let's clear the air first, okay?"

Lee nodded. "I mean, no offence Shell, but you just killed someone. I'm more than happy to let bygones be bygones."

"That's not what I mean." Shell bit her lip, struggling to meet Lee's eye. "Basically, I lied about what I said. My dad didn't hear anything, and he certainly doesn't have any recordings."

Lee's brows knitted in confusion.

"There's no way he could've called the police yet," Shell rushed on, "because he doesn't have anything to show them."

Comprehension dawned on Lee's face. "Oh. But you did record something. You showed me. I heard my voice on it."

"Yeah, it is a voice recorder, but it isn't connected to my dad's cloud or any cloud account for that matter. It's an old fashioned one from twenty years ago, he never gets rid of old stuff. Everything we talked about last night and this morning is just saved on it."

Lee blinked in surprise but said nothing. Aware she still had his knife and had already used it as a weapon, he wisely held his council. They started to walk again, slower this time.

"I don't know why I said it," Shell admitted. "I was thinking on my feet. I was relieved that I finally knew the truth, but I was also pissed off at you for lying about it the way you did," She exhaled sharply. "I mean, don't get me wrong, I'm still pissed off, but at least I understand everything now. At that moment, I guess I just wanted you to feel like you couldn't hide anymore."

Shell gestured towards the riverbank. "If none of this had happened, I was gonna go home and let my dad take care of everything, if I'm being honest."

Lee rubbed the back of his neck, eyes downcast. "Well, since we're being honest, I'm not saying this to make you feel guilty or anything, but I did think about killing myself after you left."

Shell's face softened. "Fuck sake, Lee."

"I thought I'd be better off dead instead of going to prison."

Shell broke eye contact with a heavy sigh.

"But don't worry," Lee added quickly. "I changed my mind right before you called me. When all of this is done, I'm handing myself in, I promise."

Shell stared at the ground, while Lee shifted uncomfortably from one foot to the other.

Finally Shell asked, "What about your immunity from prosecution?"

"I don't think that matters if I hand myself in voluntarily."

Shell slowly nodded, eyes still downcast.

"Alright," Shell said faintly. "Fair enough."

Lee cleared his throat. "And I am sorry that I threatened you. I really wasn't thinking clearly-"

"I know, I know," Shell interjected gently. "The important thing is that you didn't go through with it. Because if you had..." She trailed off, staring towards Robbie's body a short distance away.

Lee followed Shell's gaze to the dark shape laid out on the grass.

"...Things would be very different for us both right now." Shell finished.

Their eyes met again. "I'm sorry, Shell." Lee said quietly.

"I'm sorry too. If anything, I should be thanking you," Shell reached into her bag and pulled out Lee's bloodied steak knife. "For saving my life."

Lee nodded, a thin smile touching his lips.

As Shell returned the knife to her bag, Lee added, "Actually, you saved *both* our lives."

Shell considered Lee a moment before opening her arms out slightly, gesturing a hug.

Lee's brows shot up in surprise. "You sure?"

Shell nodded. Lee approached cautiously and they embraced in a brief, awkward hug before stepping back. Shell tilted her head towards Robbie's body.

"I'm gonna warn you though," Shell said, resuming their slow walk. "It's not a pretty sight."

Lee fell into step beside her. "Before or after you killed him?"

Shell laughed softly. "Have you ever seen a dead body before, Lee?"

"Yeah, once," Lee's smile faded. "When I was homeless. Her name was Rose. She was old and I didn't really know her that well, but she was lovely, always friendly to everyone she met. She either died in her sleep or she froze to death. Horrible way to go, she didn't deserve that. I was the one who found her."

Lee took a breath, not realising just how long it had been since he had thought about Rose, let alone talk about her.

"It was weird though, because she didn't look real, so it was easier to deal with, if that makes sense? She didn't look human."

"Yeah, I get it. I'm really sorry." Shell offered, with sincerity.

"It's alright, thank you." Lee cocked his head curiously at Shell. "How about you?"

"My mum. She had a seizure in front of me when I was eleven. Mark was there too," Shell's voice was distant, her eyes fixed ahead. "He told me to call my dad while he tried CPR, but yeah, she didn't make it."

"Oh God. I'm so sorry to hear that." Lee said gently.

Shell shrugged it off. "It's okay."

They walked a few paces in silence before Lee spoke again. "Now that you mention it, I don't think I ever heard Mark talk about your mum."

"None of us did really."

"How come?"

Shell's jaw tensed. "Too painful, I guess."

Lee nodded in understanding and they continued on towards the dark hulk of Robbie's body. As they drew closer, Lee made a small noise of disgust. Blood pooled thickly around Robbie's neck, seeping across the grass.

"Jesus Christ."

"Are you alright, yeah?" Shell asked.

"Yeah, yeah, I just can't believe what I'm looking at."

They stopped a few feet away, Shell surveying the scene with an impassive expression. "Do you need a minute?"

Lee shook his head, exhaling slowly through his mouth. "No, no, I'm good. I'm glad it's his body I'm looking at though and not yours."

Shell walked around to the other side of Robbie and stood facing Lee, the heavy corpse sprawled between them.

"Are you sure you wanna help?" Shell asked bluntly. "Because once you touch his body, that's it, there's no going back."

Lee met Shell's eye with a solemn nod. "I mean, I'm already here."

"Lee, I'm serious. You can't back out when you do this. You know he's got family in MI5. This type of thing won't be brushed under the carpet. Even though I killed him in self defence, it's probably gonna be a lifetime of bullshit for us both. This is your last chance to walk away."

Lee dragged a hand over his mouth, eyes darting around the deserted landscape. Then he sighed. "Well, what exactly do you want me to do? What's the plan?"

Shell toed the ground where blood had started to cake and harden. "I think we've got no choice. We have to destroy the body."

Lee frowned. "Why can't we just leave everything as it is and say he tried to kill you and you fought back? I mean, that *is* the truth."

"Lee," Shell said sharply. "MI5. Robbie got away with murdering a woman because they got involved. The police either turned a blind eye or they got paid off, one or the other. Robbie's family can easily create their own narrative here. That's what we're dealing with, so we need to do something while we have the chance."

With an impatient huff, Lee turned towards the Mondeo. Shell followed his gaze to the car, petrol fumes wafting thickly from the exterior.

Shell continued. "Lee. I stabbed my ex boyfriend in the neck in the middle of nowhere on a cold Saturday morning a few weeks before Halloween. True crime podcasts will have a field day with that narrative."

Lee looked down at the body and noticed something on the grass above Robbie's head. "Are they swimming goggles?"

Shell bent down to pick up the goggles. She stood back up and examined them while wiping the blood off with her top. "Yeah. He knew I had pepper spray. His family were following me and then he caught up. This is exactly what I'm talking about."

Shell presented the goggles to Lee. He looked at them in her hand as she continued, "This. He came prepared, Lee. His family tried to help him kill his ex-girlfriend. If I didn't have your knife, I'd be going up in smoke right now."

Shell lowered her hand and dropped the goggles onto the grass. "This is why you need to understand. It's all or nothing."

"What else am I gonna do, Shell? Spend another two years hiding in hotels on my own?"

Lee sighed. "Mark's dead. I don't care what the others think about me now. I already said I'm handing myself in after this anyway, so what's the point?" His voice was laced with a certain acceptance to his fate. "I've spent the last two years regretting walking out on Mark when he needed me the most. I'm not about to make the same mistake with his sister."

Shell tried holding back her smile. "Thank you, Lee."

"Besides," Lee said in a forced cheerful tone, "it's not every day you get to cut up a dead body!"

"Well, I don't think we could do that."

"What do you mean? I thought that's what you want us to do?"

"No, I said we need to destroy the body," Shell clarified. "We'll have to do what he was gonna do to me."

Shell followed the stench of petrol, glancing at the Mondeo. "We'll have to burn him."

"Oh, okay. So we're skipping the church service and going straight to the crematorium?" Lee said, in a vain attempt at lightening the dour situation.

Shell gave Lee a small smile, shrugged, then walked towards the car to take a look at the back seats through the open passenger door. Lee followed her.

"He already doused the car with petrol, so we'll have to pick him up and chuck him in the back seat. The two of us should manage that." Shell affirmed.

Lee nodded, not really paying attention to Shell's idea. "Yeah, it does smell like a petrol station around here."

"So you good with that, yeah?" Shell asked, realising that Lee hadn't been listening. "Picking him up and putting him in the car?"

"Yeah," Lee answered, unassuredly. He looked back at Robbie, realising just how large of a task it would be. "He looks like a heavy fucker."

Shell winced. "Yeah, he is," A visible shiver passed through her. "Can't even think about it."

Shell walked slowly back to Robbie's lifeless body, with Lee following closely behind. She stopped and looked down at Robbie, sprawled face up on the dirty grass. His skin had already started taking on a grey pallor.

"Right, we need to do this quickly," Shell said, her voice steady despite the macabre task that lay before them. "If I grab his legs, you'll have to pick him up from under his shoulders. Can you do that?"

Lee shifted his weight, hesitation playing across his face. "Oh, I thought we were just gonna grab a limb each."

"Well if he didn't weigh a tonne, then yeah, but one of us has to support his weight from the top while the other levels him out." Shell squatted down and took hold of Robbie's ankles. His pants were stained with blood that had squirted from the fatal wound in his neck.

Lee remained motionless, his mind racing while watching Shell's efforts.

Shell looked up, her eyebrows raised. "Come on, what you waiting for?"

Lee acted fidgety, like a moth beating its wings against a light. Every time he stepped closer towards Robbie's head, he stopped for a brief moment, unable to make contact.

Shell's patience was starting to wear thin. "Lee, we haven't got all day."

"Just give me a sec." Lee stuttered, shifting from foot to foot. Finally he stilled himself and took a deep breath.

"Lee. There's no way I can pick him up from that end. I'm not strong enough, so you'll have to do it, okay?" Shell's voice had softened slightly, but her expression remained resolute.

"It's not that." Lee met Shell's gaze.

"Is it the blood?"

"No, I don't think this is the right idea." Lee's face clouded over.

Shell released her grasp on Robbie's ankles and stood, wiping her hands on her top. "What are you talking about?"

"This. All of it. I just don't think we should do this." Lee's words came out in a rush.

Shell crossed her arms, arching an eyebrow. "Lee, we just said that we would–"

Lee held up a hand. "—No, *you* just said. I don't think you've thought this through enough."

"Well. The floor is all yours, Sherlock." Shell's words dripped sarcasm.

Lee glanced briefly at the ground before stepping away from Robbie's body. His eyes flickered to the Mondeo parked nearby, then he walked over to Shell, stopping a few feet away. He scratched the back of his head.

"Right, you can get away with this, even if his family tries any of their bullshit."

Shell's stance softened somewhat, but remained unconvinced. "How?"

"How many people know that you've been following me for two weeks?" Lee asked.

Shell considered for a moment. "My dad. That's it. Oh, and MI5, so I'd say quite a few."

"You have proof of it though, don't you?" Lee pressed on eagerly, slightly stuttering. "The journal? You said you were writing everything down, where I was going and all that?"

"Yeah, that's right."

"And not to mention you have an entire conversation recorded in my hotel room last night and this morning." Excitement crept into Lee's voice.

Confusion clouded Shell's features. "What's your point, Lee?"

"Everything you have, it gives you a solid alibi. When was the last time you spoke with your dad?"

"This morning–" Shell hesitated. "Well, I didn't actually speak to him. I left him a voicemail just before Robbie kidnapped me."

Lee nodded. "What did you say?"

Shell cast her mind back. "Er, I told him I was leaving the hotel and that I'd be back home before seven."

"Perfect!" Lee exclaimed. "So not only do you have a journal that documents our every move, but you also have audio proof of us in my hotel room on the tenth and eleventh of October – and there's even a voicemail that gives specific times and everything!"

"You seem to be forgetting something, Lee. All of that just proves I was in the area when Robbie was killed." Shell bit her lip.

"Precisely!" Lee grinned, eyes lighting up.

Shell shook her head slowly. "I don't follow."

"We have proof that we did - and said - everything from two weeks ago, right up until the moment Robbie kidnapped you. He drove you all the way out here, you called me, I came to get you." Lee spread his hands wide, as if the simplicity of the situation was obvious.

"Right?" Shell still looked bemused.

"MI5 can even back all of that up. They knew that you had pepper spray in your handbag... there was never any mention of a knife." Lee raised his eyebrows meaningfully.

Slowly, Shell uncrossed her arms, her face dawning with understanding. "No, wait..."

Lee nodded eagerly. "That's right. I killed Robbie with my steak knife, not you."

Shell's expression changed in an instant, her eyes flashing. "No, Lee, I can't let you take the blame for this. You'd spend the rest of your life behind bars."

Lee threw his hands up in frustration. "For what? For saving my best friend's sister? For killing a psychopath?"

"I don't care, Lee. We're not doing it." Shell set her jaw stubbornly.

"Why not?" Lee demanded.

"Because!" Shell turned her back on Lee, wrapping her arms around herself.

Lee tried a different angle. "I'm already going to prison anyway, Shell. I may as well go in for something that actually adds credit to my name. Prisoners will respect me, maybe even word will get back to Paul and Freddie and the others. If everyone knew I got sent down for saving Mark's sister, I'd be treated like a hero!"

Shell whirled to face Lee. "I said no!"

Lee ran a hand through the remains of his hair in agitation. "Shell, seriously!"

Shell jabbed a finger towards Lee. "No! I'm not making an innocent man go to prison for something he didn't do! I can't have that on my conscience..." Her voice cracked as she froze.

Shell had a moment of realisation regarding Lee's entire situation. She finally understood that she had overstepped his boundaries with wild accusations about his character that were simply untrue. She could almost feel Mark's disappointment coming from beyond the grave.

A perplexed look passed over Lee's face and he fell silent, not knowing how to respond.

Shell took a shuddering breath as she attempted to rein in her emotions. She scrubbed at her face with both hands for a few seconds before speaking again.

"I'm sorry, Lee. I'm sorry."

Shell stared down at Robbie's lifeless body sprawled on the ground, crimson blood pooled under his head. Her gaze lifted to the Mondeo parked haphazardly on the riverbank, then shifted to Lee, who stood solemnly beside her.

"You were willing to go to prison for me today, not just once but twice," Shell said, her voice low but firm. "Both of them over things that you had no control of."

Lee pressed his lips together, strangling back the words perched on the tip of his tongue.

"A friend of yours who became a copper, confronted you with an impossible situation," Shell continued, her eyes piercing Lee's. "You had to either risk being branded as a traitor by warning Mark about the raid, or accept police protection so everyone else would go to prison."

Shell paused, shaking her head faintly. "Honestly, I don't blame you for the choice you made. You did nothing wrong," Her voice caught. "It was a lose-lose for you anyway. That's what Mark was trying to tell me."

Shell's stoic facade crumbled as tears welled in her eyes. Lee stood frozen, unsure how to respond.

"Mark was just trying to protect you," Shell went on, swiping at the wet streaks on her cheeks. "He knew you'd never go out your way to betray him or anyone else. He knew how loyal you are. I mean, for God's sake, you already proved that by saying you killed Robbie when you had fuck all to do with it!"

A sob escaped Shell's lips and Lee stepped forward, wrapping her in his arms. "Hey, hey, it's alright, come on, come on."

Shell cried into Lee's shoulder, her body shaking. "I'm so sorry, Lee, for everything. I should have listened to Mark, I should have trusted him. We should've left you alone."

Lee gently grasped Shell's shoulders, easing out of the embrace to meet her watery gaze. "It's okay. Honestly, it's fine."

Shell swiped at her cheek with the back of her hand. "It's not! I've been nothing but a cold hearted bitch to you."

"Alright, so what? You had every right to be," Lee countered gently. "You didn't owe me anything. As far as you were aware, I was just some guy on the run spending your brother's money while he was behind bars. I knew exactly how I came across - I lied to you, I got angry at you, I nearly hit you for fuck sake. You don't owe me anything, Shell."

Shell's tears ceased as she studied Lee's face. When she spoke, her voice was steady and sure. "Okay. This is what we're gonna do. We're both gonna leave."

Confusion etched over Lee's face. "Leave?"

"Yeah. We're gonna get in your car, drive back to the hotel, I'm gonna get my dad's car and then we're gonna go our separate ways."

"What about Robbie?" Lee asked, gesturing to the body.

Shell's eyes followed. "Fuck Robbie. He had it coming."

A hint of a smile played on Lee's lips but quickly faded. "Where's all this come from? What about MI5?"

Shell met Lee's uncertain look with calm resolve. "You're right, Lee. We'll just tell the truth. I stabbed Robbie in self defence after he kidnapped me and tried to burn me alive. I don't give a fuck what anyone else says. God is on my side, that's all that matters."

At that moment, the phone in her handbag trilled loudly. Cursing under her breath, Shell rummaged hurriedly for the device, checking the name flashing on the screen.

"It's my dad!" Shell answered the call. "Dad! Did you get my message?"

Lee stood motionless, watching Shell pace slowly back and forth.

"Yes, I know what time it is. Did you listen to my voicemail?...Yeah, his name is Peter Dean. He's the one who set Mark up." Shell explained to her dad.

Lee remained slightly anxious as to where Shell was leading the conversation.

"Lee? No, he didn't have anything to do with it. Mark was right...You can't. Because it didn't record anything."

Lee slowly raised his hands behind his head in disbelief.

"Well, it's not my fault, I told you it was too old. We should've used a modern one but you didn't listen, did you?" Shell said in exasperation.

"No, you'll just have to take my word for it. I don't have it anymore. I smashed it up because it didn't work. It pissed me off," Shell's lips curved into a faint, sly smile as her eyes met Lee's. "But I remember everything that was said, clear as day. Dad, it doesn't matter—we've got our guy now. Lee is completely innocent."

Shell gave Lee a knowing nod. "Okay, yeah, I'll tell you everything when I get home in about an hour. There's a lot that you need to prepare yourself for..." Her eyes darted towards Robbie's body. "...You'll understand when I tell you. Okay. Love you too, bye."

Lee felt a swell of gratitude and affection for this headstrong, crafty woman. As Shell ended the call, she retrieved the small voice recorder from her handbag and marched purposefully to the river's edge.

In one smooth motion, she hurled the device into the murky water.

When she turned to Lee, Shell's eyes glinted with feisty determination.

Lee couldn't keep the look of shock mixed with appreciation off his face. "I can't believe you did that."

Shell shrugged. "You coming or what?" She headed for the Fiesta, Lee falling in step behind her.

Just before they both approached the car, Lee stopped and grabbed Shell's attention.

"Oh wait, hang on a sec," Lee said while he began fumbling his hand in his unzipped trouser pocket, retrieving the gold ring that read '*United Kingham*'.

"I meant to give it back at the hotel this morning," Lee explained, holding it out to Shell. "Before... well, before everything happened."

Shell accepted the ring, clenching it tightly in her fist. "Thank you."

Their eyes locked for a long moment before Lee walked up to the car and opened the driver's door, sliding into the seat. Shell took one last look towards the riverbank before she walked up to the passenger door and opened it.

Sitting inside the vehicle, Shell turned to Lee before he started the engine. "Hang on."

"What's up?" Lee asked.

Shell forced out a bleak giggle as she gently placed the palm of her hand over her black eye. "Do you have any paracetamol? I've got a banging headache now."

"Yeah, yeah, of course, wait there."

"Thanks, Lee."

He quickly exited the car and made his way to the boot, being careful to not make too much noise as he fumbled around the contents of his gym bag to retrieve the medicine.

Shell closed her eyes and leant her head back onto the head rest. She couldn't help but appreciate her new found lease on life. A life that she and her dad could finally enjoy.

She clasped the gold ring in her hand. The verse of Luke 12:48 was on repeat in her mind. After everything she had been through, she knew in her heart that Mark could finally rest in peace.

As Lee returned to the driver's seat, he handed over the medicine to Shell before he started the engine and steered them both back to The Puppet Master Hotel.

A new understanding had passed between Shell Kingham and Lee Barker. They were now united against whatever lay ahead.

Acknowledgements

Strictly based on those who played their part in helping make this book come to fruition;

My Dad gave me useful tips regarding prose, proofreading, and also spent countless hours reading through the story to make sure everything checked out. Thank you Dad.

My Mum's constant love and support gave me all the encouragement I needed to continue writing and I can't thank you enough for that Mum. Love you both.

Thank you for reading **Much Is Required**. I wish you good health in body & mind.

9 781803 819488